OXFORD CHILDREN'S MYTHS AND LEGENDS

JAMES REEVES

❖

STORIES FROM
ENGLAND

OXFORD
UNIVERSITY PRESS

OXFORD
UNIVERSITY PRESS

Great Clarendon Street, Oxford OX2 6DP

Oxford University Press is a department of the University of Oxford.
It furthers the University's objective of excellence in research, scholarship,
and education by publishing worldwide in

Oxford   New York

Auckland   Cape Town   Dar es Salaam   Hong Kong   Karachi
Kuala Lumpur   Madrid   Melbourne   Mexico City   Nairobi
New Delhi   Shanghai   Taipei   Toronto

With offices in

Argentina   Austria   Brazil   Chile   Czech Republic   France   Greece
Guatemala   Hungary   Italy   Japan   Poland   Portugal   Singapore
South Korea   Switzerland   Thailand   Turkey   Ukraine   Vietnam

Oxford is a registered trade mark of Oxford University Press
in the UK and in certain other countries

© James Reeves 1954

The moral rights of the author have been asserted

Database right Oxford University Press (maker)

First published as *English Fables & Fairy Tales* 1954
First published in this paperback edition 2013

British Library Cataloguing in Publication Data

Data available

ISBN: 978-0-19-273660-4

1 3 5 7 9 10 8 6 4 2

Printed in Great Britain

Paper used in the production of this book is a natural,
recyclable product made from wood grown in sustainable forests.
The manufacturing process conforms to the environmental
regulations of the country of origin.

To My Mother

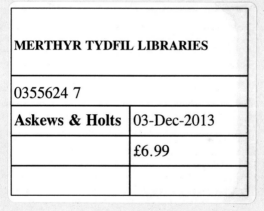

CONTENTS

JACK HANNAFORD

———— ❖ ————

There was once an old soldier named Jack Hannaford. For over twenty years he had been at the wars in the Low Countries, fighting and marching, sleeping in tent and barn, stealing a goose here and a guinea there to make up for a soldier's poor victuals and small pay. He was not a rogue by nature, but the wars had turned him into one, for he possessed nothing of his own, and had never learned a trade.

When he got back to England, he was thin and ragged, with a patch over one eye and very little hair on top of his head. He was rusty and weather-beaten and the brightest thing about him was his one bright eye. Off he went to tramp through the county of Suffolk and make what he could by beggary and trickery and such-like ways.

Now at that time there was, living in the county of Suffolk, a foolish farmer and his foolish good wife. Fat and rosy they were, for they lived well, though they had but little money to spend. Yet there were always eggs in the larder, plenty of butter and milk, a fat cockerel ready for the pot, and a fine ham swinging from a hook in the kitchen. In all his time the foolish

1

farmer had saved ten gold guineas, and these he kept in a pocket of his brown cloth jacket.

One day he had to ride to town to see a lawyer about a cottage that stood on his land, but he was afraid he might be robbed, so he left the ten gold guineas with his wife.

'Wife,' says he, 'I shall be back before nightfall, but I may be stopped on the road and robbed. Here are my ten guineas. Look after them for me and keep them safe.'

'Oh dear me,' says his wife, 'I don't like this at all, for you know I am a foolish body, and never could keep money.'

But she took the money and wrapped it in a handkerchief and wrapped the handkerchief in a bit of sacking and put the bundle in a hole above the chimney.

'Now whoever comes,' thinks she, 'would never dream of looking there for the money, so surely it will be safe and sound.'

Well, the farmer went off on his horse, and when he got near the town an old soldier with a patch over one eye met him on the road, but the farmer took no notice of him and went on his way. His wife, meanwhile, had put on her apron and taken up her broom, and she set to work to sweep up the farmhouse.

After a time she looked out of the window and saw the same old soldier who had met her husband on the road an hour or two back. She thought of the ten gold guineas in the handkerchief, but she knew they were safe in their hole above the chimney. Presently there was a knock at the door, and the farmer's wife went to it and opened it, and there stood Jack Hannaford, the ragged soldier from the Low Countries.

'Good day, ma'am,' says he.

'Good day,' says she, 'and what may you be wanting?'

'Nothing but a crust of bread and a mug of water—or maybe of ale, if you have such a thing.'

'Come inside,' says she. 'I've no ale, and the crusts of bread I keep for the two black pigs; but I have a cup of new milk for you and a piece of dough-cake that's not been out of the oven above an hour.'

'Thank you, ma'am,' says Jack politely, and steps inside, remembering to limp a little to show how worn and weary he was. The good wife gave him the food and drink and he sat down by the fireplace, and they got to talking. Jack's one bright eye was peering round the room to see if there was anything silver that he might make off with if the farmer was not at home; but nothing worthwhile could he see, for the room was bare and simply furnished. Once or twice the good wife glanced up towards the hole in the chimney, but nothing was to be seen of the money in the handkerchief. She told the old soldier about the farmer her husband and about her first husband, who had been a cobbler but was dead these ten years.

'A fine man he was,' said she, 'and a good cobbler. From London he was,' she said, 'and he came out here to escape the plague. And where might you be from?'

'Why, as for me,' says Jack, 'I am from Paradise.'

'From Paradise?' says the simple wife. 'Well, fancy that! Now if you come from Paradise, perhaps you have met my first husband, for it's there he is, for sure.'

'What was his name?' asks Jack.

The good wife told him.

'Why, to be sure,' says Jack, 'he is a good friend of mine, and I know him well. A fine cobbler he is, as you say. Why, it's he who makes all the shoes for the blessed saints and angels.'

3

'Well, fancy that,' says the simple wife. 'And how is he doing now?'

'Poorly, ma'am, poorly,' says Jack, looking very sorrowful. 'He has spent his last shilling, and he hasn't money enough to buy shoe-leather to go on with his work, and it's in a bad way the saints and angels of Paradise will be if he can't get leather to mend their shoes.'

'Dear, oh dear,' says the farmer's wife, and she begins to shed tears as she thinks of her poor old husband, the cobbler from London.

'But I shall be going back there tonight,' says Jack, 'and if you had a few guineas or even only a few shillings I could give him, 'twould make him happy again for certain.'

Well, the poor wife was so upset with sorrow for the sad case of her first husband that she forgot all about her promise to the farmer to keep his guineas safe.

'Why, to be sure,' says she, 'and there is a little money hidden away, and I'll get it out this minute, if you will be so good as to take it to my poor dead husband.'

So she got up on a stool and took the bundle down from the hole above the fireplace and laid it on the table. She unwrapped the sacking, and next the handkerchief, and then she asked Jack how much he thought the cobbler needed.

'Why, ma'am,' says Jack, 'it wouldn't do to be mean in a matter like this, now would it? For I may never come this way again—indeed, I think it's very unlikely I will; and this may be your only chance of doing the poor fellow a bit of good. So why not give me all you can spare, and think no more about it?'

The simple woman hesitated no longer, but put all the ten gold guineas into the soldier's hand.

4

'Here,' says she, 'take all we have, and give it to my poor dead husband with my love and blessing. And a blessing on you too for doing an honest woman so kind a turn.'

Jack put the ten guineas into the pocket of his ragged coat, thanked the farmer's wife for her blessing, and made off as fast as he could; and the simple wife was left to get her husband's supper, for she knew he would not be long coming back from the town.

As soon as the farmer came back, she told him about the old soldier and how she had given him the money to take back to Paradise.

'Paradise!' says the farmer. 'Paradise! Why folks don't come back and forth from Paradise as if it was Ipswich Market! You're a fool, wife! You have given all my money to a common thief and a vagabond, and left me as poor as when I married you.'

The wife began to weep.

'Well, if it's a fool I am,' she sobbed, 'it's you are the bigger, for you knew I was nought but a simple woman, and you should never have left the money with me!'

'You never said a truer word, old woman. It's the biggest fool I am in all the county for trusting such a ninny as you with my money. Where's my horse? I'll catch the rogue if I drop down dead and the old horse as well!'

So the farmer ran out into the yard, jumped on his horse, and galloped away down the road that Jack had taken.

Now Jack had not gone above two miles down the road, and he was thinking what a clever fellow he had been, when he heard the sound of horse's hooves in a furious gallop.

'This'll be the farmer,' says he to himself, 'come after me

for his money. He'll take the money from me and give me a sound beating into the bargain, I shouldn't wonder. Now where shall I hide?'

But there was no time to find a hiding-place. The road was long and straight, and by now the farmer had already caught sight of him. Very quickly Jack stepped to the side of the road, lay down in the ditch, and began to look very intently up into the sky. Presently the farmer came alongside and got off his horse.

'Hallo,' said the farmer. 'What are you doing there, my fine fellow, and why do you look up into the sky?'

'Look there,' says Jack, shading his one eye with his hand.

'What is it?' asks the farmer, looking up. 'I don't see any-thing.'

'And I see a fellow flying away as fast as he can,' says Jack. 'Come and lie down here, and you'll see the same.'

'Very well,' says the farmer, 'if you'll be so good as to hold my horse, I'll lie down and take a look.'

So up jumps Jack, and the farmer gets down in the ditch and lies on his back, looking up into the sky.

'Now take a look!' cries Jack. 'Now do you see a fellow fly-ing away as fast as he can?'

And he jumps into the saddle of the farmer's horse, digs his heels in her sides, sets off at a flying gallop, and disappears down the road before ever the farmer can get to his feet. And that was the last he saw of Jack Hannaford.

Presently the sound of hooves died away in the distance. Slowly the farmer trudged home on foot, cursing himself for his foolishness. He had lost both his ten gold guineas that he had been ten years saving, and his stout brown mare into the bargain.

'My wife be no more than a fool,' said he to himself, 'but I be twice a fool—firstly, for trusting such a fool as she with the money, and next for letting such a rogue get away from under my very hand.'

And when he got home he told his wife what had happened and owned that he was the bigger fool of the two. So they sat down to supper, and after supper they both fell to laughing to think how easily they had been cheated of their money.

TATTERCOATS

❖

There was once an old lord who lived in a great castle by the sea. He was lonely, for the castle was bare and empty, and there were no young and gay people to make its great halls ring with laughter. All day the lord would pace the stone corridors or sit alone in his room looking out over the grey sea.

He had one little granddaughter, whose face he had never looked on. He hated the child from the day she was born, because on that day her mother died, and her mother had been the old lord's favourite and dearly-loved daughter. The little girl's father had gone far away over the sea to fight for the King, so it was as if she had no parents and no one to care for her—no one, that is, except her old nurse, who kept her in her room, fed her with scraps of food from her grandfather's table, and clothed her in whatever old and worn-out garments she could find.

Because the lord hated his granddaughter, most of the servants ill-treated her, calling her names and telling her to keep out of their way. 'Tattercoats' was the name that everyone called her, because of her clothes.

Tattercoats spent her days playing in the yard at the back of the castle or down by the lonely seashore; or else she would go off to the fields and look for the crippled goose-herd, who was her only playfellow. This was a lad a little older than she was, who had been lame from birth and lived on a farm nearby. It was his task to drive the geese every morning out of the farm-yard, over the fields, and down to the pond where they splashed and swam and dived for fish. He used to play on a little pipe, and this was Tattercoats's greatest joy—to hear the quaint tunes, merry or sad, which the goose-herd played on his pipe. Sometimes they would make her think of the fairies in the woods, sometimes they would make her think of foreign coun-tries, or far-off mountains and rivers; sometimes the music was so light and merry that it made her dance. Even the goose-herd would dance, now and again, in his clumsy way. So the days passed in spring and summer. In winter, when the evenings were long, Tattercoats would draw close to the fire in her old nurse's room and make her tell stories of knights and ladies, battles and giants, or of the fairies who play by the sea and fly invisibly through the air. Tattercoats would sit and listen for as long as her nurse would let her, gazing into the fire till her cheeks were warm and her eyes shone bright, and at last she began to nod and her nurse yawned and said she could tell no more tales and the little girl must go to bed. Yet much as she loved to hear stories, Tattercoats was happiest when everyone forgot about her and she could slip away and find her friend the goose-herd, who played such magical tunes on his pipe; and they would talk and play all the long summer evenings, or else Tattercoats would try to remember a story to tell the goose-herd, or the goose-herd would pipe for her to dance. Then the world would be forgotten, and the great bare castle, and the unkind servants, and her grandfather whom she had never seen.

The years went by, and the old lord got older and sadder; and now he would scarcely even walk about his castle, but would sit all day and all night by the window overlooking the sad sea, till his long white beard grew down over his knees and over his feet and began to twine round the legs of his chair. And the tears would fall from his eyes as he thought of his favourite daughter who was dead. So, weeping and thinking, he sat there, as the years went slowly by.

Then one day the King came to visit the town nearby, and he sent invitations to all the lords and nobles and their ladies to come to a great ball. His son, the Prince, had come of age, and it was known that he was looking for a bride. Now, when a king sends invitations, they are not so much invitations as commands; and a command came to the old lord in the castle by the sea to come to the ball in the town and do honour to the royal court. So a milk-white horse was saddled and bridled; and the lord sent for a barber with a great pair of scissors to cut away the long white beard that bound him to the chair. Then he put on fine clothes and went down to the courtyard to mount the milk-white horse and ride to town. It happened that Tattercoats, who was now a fine, big girl, graceful and sweet, though still dressed in tatters, was talking with the old nurse in her room upstairs. And when she heard the horse jingling and clattering in the courtyard below, she asked the nurse what was to do.

'The King has ordered a great ball to be held in town,' said the nurse, 'and he has commanded your grandfather to attend it. If you look out of the window, you will see him.'

'Oh, how I should love to go to the King's ball!' said Tattercoats. 'Go to my grandfather and plead with him to take me—please, please, dear nurse, before it is too late.'

Just then the old man strode stiffly into the courtyard and mounted the horse, helped by a groom and a stable-boy.

'Is that my grandfather?' said Tattercoats. 'How handsome he looks in his fine clothes. Oh, how I wish he would take me!'

'I would never dare ask him,' said the nurse. 'Besides, it is too late now. He would be gone before my old bones would take me downstairs.'

Even as she spoke, the groom handed the lord the reins, and the milk-white horse carried him away through the castle gate. Tattercoats watched him till he was out of sight, then she turned from the window and began to cry.

'My first ball,' she sobbed. 'It might have been my first ball. Now I shall never go to one. I have lost my chance, and it won't come again. And all because *you* wouldn't go and speak to my grandfather!'

She turned angrily to the nurse, who answered:

'Now, hush, my dear. Balls and festivities aren't for the likes of you. Don't turn on your old nurse. *I* could do nothing for you. He won't listen to *me*. Even if I'd have spoken to him, he'd never have taken you. It's as much as my place is worth to look after you the way I do. So don't give yourself airs, young mistress. I do what I can for you, but a miracle-worker I never was, and don't you forget it.'

Tattercoats stopped crying as quickly as she had started and asked her nurse to forgive her.

'There, nurse,' she said, 'don't you scold me, or I shan't

have a friend in the world. I didn't mean it, truly I didn't. It's not your fault. I don't want to go to the silly old ball and see all the lords and ladies giving themselves airs in their fine new clothes—and don't you forget *that*.'

All the same, as she wandered out through the courtyard into the green fields, which were bright with the afternoon sunlight, she thought how much she would have liked to have just one look at all those proud faces and splendid dresses, to see the King nodding kindly as the lords bowed to him and the ladies curtsied, to hear the grave music and the laughing and whispering, and perhaps even catch sight of the Prince himself as he moved, handsome and stately, among the dancers.

So she dreamed to herself as she loitered along the path, and she hardly noticed her young friend the goose-herd as he limped up to greet her, followed by his little flock of grey geese. He played a few plaintive notes on his little pipe and said:

'A penny for your thoughts, Tattercoats. Would you like a merry tune to make you dance, or a sad one to make you cry?'

'I want to dance,' said Tattercoats, 'but not here. I wanted so much to go to town to the King's ball, but I haven't been asked, and that's the long and short of it.'

'You want to go to town,' said the goose-herd. 'Then to town you shall go, and I and my geese will go with you. It's not so far for a tall strong walker like yourself or even a hobbling piper like me.'

So off they went down the white road, and the goose-herd made the distance seem no distance at all by playing his merriest, sweetest tunes; and soon Tattercoats forgot all her sadness and was dancing along by his side as pleasantly as ever.

13

When they were near the town, they heard the sound of horses' hooves on the road behind them, and a tall handsome young man on a black horse came up beside them.

'Are you going to town?' he asked, bending over his horse's neck. 'If so, I'll go along with you, for you seem good company.'

'Why yes, sir,' answered the goose-herd. 'We are going to town to see the fine people arrive for the King's ball. Go with us, and welcome.'

The young man jumped down from his horse and walked beside Tattercoats, while the goose-herd followed after, striking up a tune on his pipe.

Then the young man stopped still and looked at Tattercoats. 'Do you know who I am?' he asked.

'Why no, sir,' said she. 'How should I?'

'I am the Prince,' said he, 'and I am on my way to my father's ball. Let me look at you a minute.'

Then, as the Prince began to gaze at Tattercoats's face, the goose-herd played a new tune, a sweet and strange tune with magic in it. Tattercoats scarcely heard it, for she was looking into the Prince's eyes; and the Prince scarcely heard, for he was thinking that never in his life had he seen a fairer face. He did not see the girl's tattered clothes, bare feet, and untidy hair—he only saw her sweet, shy face, and for a while he said nothing.

Then at last he spoke.

'What is your name?' he asked.

'I am called Tattercoats,' she said. 'That is the only name I ever had.'

'I am the Prince,' he said, 'and tonight I look for a bride.

14

I never saw anyone who moved my heart as you do. Tattercoats, will you marry me and be my Princess?'

Tattercoats could say nothing. Instead, she only looked up at the Prince. His horse moved one hoof, a little impatiently, and the goose-herd's music was still.

'I ask you again,' said the Prince. 'Tattercoats, will you be my bride?'

Then Tattercoats smiled and shook her head.

'No,' she said. 'You are making fun of me. I am no wife for a Prince. Ride off to your great ball and choose a bride from among the fine court ladies.'

'I am in earnest,' said the Prince, 'but if you say no, I can see from your face that you mean it. If you will not be my bride, will you at least come to the ball? Listen: I ask you to go to the ball at midnight, just as you are, with the goose-herd here, and his pipe, and all his geese. Will you come?'

Tattercoats looked at him.

'Perhaps,' she said. 'Perhaps not. I don't know.'

The Prince said nothing more, but mounted his black horse and galloped away towards the town.

The goose-herd played a few notes on his pipe and came up to Tattercoats.

'Take fortune when it comes,' he said. 'Let's follow him.'

So off they went together into the town.

Never had the lords and ladies of that country seen a more splendid ball. All the townsfolk gathered to watch the arrival of the guests, some on horseback and some in carriages. The great hall was lit up by a thousand candles, which were reflected in the polished floor; at one end of the hall a platform supported two thrones, on which the King and the Queen received the guests. At the other end, a lofty gallery held the musicians. Two great doors led into the banqueting hall, where rich food and wines were served. Round the walls were comfortable chairs for the older people and for those not dancing. On the terrace, those who found the ballroom overheated strolled in the cool of the evening, talking and laughing with not a care in the world. The musicians played as never before; all were gay but a little anxious, for this was the night when the King's eldest son was expected to choose his bride. Perhaps he had already made his choice; perhaps none of the young ladies of his father's court would please him. How many proud ladies hid their secret hopes and fears under their light-hearted chatter and careless smiles!

The evening passed all too quickly for the throng of dancers, and still nothing was said of the Prince's choice. After all, then, he had not made up his mind. So it was thought by many. Then, just as midnight had finished striking from the great clock on the town hall, there was a flurry at the entrance to the ballroom, and the oddest sight they had ever seen greeted the courtiers' eyes. A strange procession entered as the music ceased and the lords and ladies began to leave the ballroom floor. In front came a girl clad in tattered country clothes, and behind her was a crippled goose-herd followed by nine cackling geese. What a sight to behold at the King's ball! At first the courtiers were dumb with amazement, then some began to talk and whisper, and others laughed out loud. But their laughter changed once more into silence as the Prince stepped forward and took the girl by the hand, leading her fearlessly up to the platform on which his father and mother were enthroned.

'Father,' he said, 'this is Tattercoats. If she will have me, it is she I wish to marry. What do you say?'

The King looked at the face of Tattercoats long and kindly.

'My son,' he said, 'you have chosen well. If this young lady is as good as she is beautiful, she will make you a wonderful Princess.'

'The young lady is very lovely,' said the Queen, 'but something will have to be done about her clothes.'

'And what does the lady say?' asked the King. 'Has she consented?'

'If you all wish it,' said Tattercoats in scarcely more than a whisper, 'I will be the Prince's bride.'

Then, in the silence that followed, the goose-herd put his pipe to his lips and began to play a strange tune that none had ever heard before. Instantly, Tattercoats's ragged clothes were changed into robes of shining white, with tiny diamonds sparkling upon them and a train of rose-coloured silk hanging from the shoulders. The nine geese were turned into nine page boys in suits of blue. They gathered up Tattercoats's silken train and bore it behind her as the Prince led her down the hall to begin the dance. The goose-herd's strange tune was lost in the sound of the music from the gallery, and the Prince and his bride began the dance.

That is the story of how Tattercoats became the Princess of all the land, and even the most jealous mothers agreed that she and the Prince were a well-matched pair. The King proclaimed that it was his and the Queen's pleasure that their eldest son should be betrothed to Tattercoats; and when the news was known, there was rejoicing in all the towns and villages. Bonfires were lit, bells were rung, and a public holiday was announced.

Amidst all that rejoicing there was one sad heart, the heart of the old lord, the grandfather of Tattercoats. For he never forgot his sorrow, and when the ball was over, he rode home to the castle by the sea, where he sat for the rest of his days by the window till his beard grew long and twisting once more, and the tears streamed from his eyes down his ancient and wrinkled cheeks.

As for the goose-herd, when Tattercoats had danced her first dance with the Prince, she looked round for her old play-fellow, but he was nowhere to be found. She sent out into all the countryside, but he was never heard of again. Yet sometimes country people, going home late, would fancy they heard the sweet, strange notes of his pipe behind a hedge or among the trees. But others said it must be the fairies, or perhaps just their fancy. Whether Tattercoats ever thought of him again I do not know, but she did not forget her old nurse, whom she brought with her on the day of her marriage to live in the palace of the Prince, her husband.

JOHNNY GLOKE

—— ❖ ——

Johnny Gloke was a tailor. All day he would sit cross-legged on the table in his shop, cutting and snipping, patching and sewing; making coats for ladies, suits for gentlemen, uniforms for soldiers. One day he got tired of tailoring and decided he was meant for some better fate, so he went into the field behind his shop and lay down to think about it. What should he do? He thought about playing the fiddle, but decided he was too old to learn; he thought about becoming a great general, but decided he was too much of a coward for soldiering; he thought about sailing the world in a merchant ship, but where was he to get a ship from? And as he thought, the day grew warmer and the flies began to settle on his legs and tickle his bare feet. So, hardly thinking what he was doing, he gave a great blow with the flat of his hand and killed a whole army of flies.

'Now that shows that I'm no ordinary man,' he said.

> *'Well done, Johnny Gloke—*
> *Fifty flies at one stroke!'*

How pleased he was with himself! What a fellow he must

be to kill all those flies at one stroke! Never before had he managed to kill *one* fly, let alone fifty. So up he rose, went indoors, locked the shop, put on his boots, took from the wall a rusty sword that had belonged to one of his ancestors, and set off to show the world what a great hero he was.

Johnny tramped along for a good way until he came to a notice posted up at the crossroads, and this is what it said:

REWARD!

To any man who is brave enough to slay
TWO GIANTS
and rid the country of their noisome and
dangerous presence there will be given
FIFTY THOUSAND POUNDS
AND THE HAND OF
THE KING'S ONLY DAUGHTER
in marriage.

Champions must present themselves at the
Royal Palace.

By order of HIS MAJESTY THE KING

Johnny sat down and thought about this. The idea of the fifty thousand pounds and the King's daughter in marriage appealed to him, but he was not sure whether he was any good at slaying giants. Then he gripped his rusty blade tightly in his right hand, got up from the ground, and strode on.

'After all,' he said, 'I have killed fifty flies. That is not a bad start. A man cannot be a great hero without taking some risks. At least I can find out how fierce these giants are. Perhaps they are not very terrible ones.'

'It wasn't me,' said the other giant.

'It must have been. Who else could it have been? Stand farther off, and take more care.'

He went on with his work. Johnny stooped and picked up another pebble. He threw it as hard as he could. It was not a round pebble like the first, but a three-cornered one with sharp, flinty points. It caught the ten-foot giant just behind the right ear. He roared with pain and turned ferociously on his companion.

'Now look here!' he shouted. 'If you do that once more, it'll be the end of you, do you hear? I believe you're doing it on purpose. Always were a spiteful little fellow. Only just you do it again—just you *dare* do it again!'

The third time Johnny hit him just behind the left ear. The giant roared like a whole herd of bulls and threw a log at the other giant. His aim was bad, and he missed. The log fell into the bog with a splash that could be heard half a mile away. Then the bigger giant sprang on the smaller one and beat him on the head with his fist. The smaller giant hit back, and shouted:

'It wasn't me that hit you, but if you want a fight, I'm game. Come on!'

So they turned their backs on each other and walked ten yards apart. Then they faced each other again and rushed together. The noise was like the noise of a mountain falling. It was the most tremendous fight that had ever been seen. Johnny trembled in his hollow tree, and poor folk in cottages miles around shut themselves in tight, fearing the end of the world had come. For three hours the giants fought. They banged and trounced each other for all they were worth. They roared like elephants and hammered each other till the blood flowed and the whole wood shook. All the birds in the wood flew away and did not return to their nests at all that year. But at last the two monsters began to tire. They were bruised all over and breathing hard. They stopped fighting and sat down at the edge of the bog looking very sorry for one another.

'I'm so worn out,' said one, 'that a child could lead me with a string.'

'And I'm so weary,' said the other, 'that an old woman could push me along with a feather.'

'Is that so?' said Johnny Gloke to himself. 'Then this is the moment I've been waiting for.'

So saying, he rushed out from his hiding-place and charged at the giants with his rusty sword. The bigger giant scarcely heard Johnny coming before his head was cut off; the other had just strength enough to jump up, but he fell back into the bog till only his head showed above the water. So Johnny had no difficulty in cutting it off too. Then he pushed his sword into his belt and seized the two heads, one in each hand. They were so heavy that he could hardly stagger back to the King's palace with them.

That night, there were scenes of wild rejoicing all over the land. The giants were slain, and the people could go in freedom and without fear once more. Johnny never explained exactly how he had outwitted the giants, and people supposed that the terrible noise they had heard for three hours had been the noise of his fight with them.

'What a hero indeed!' they said. 'However could he stand up to them, and he such a little fellow, no bigger than a ladies' tailor!'

So Johnny got the Princess for a wife, and with the fifty thousand pounds reward he had a splendid castle built; and there he would have been perfectly happy to spend the rest of his days in quiet and retirement. But this was not to be.

A rebellion broke out in the country, which the army was not able to put down; so of course the King turned to Johnny.

'My son,' said the King, 'some ruffians have banded themselves together and set up an outlaw camp not ten leagues distant from our very palace. Every day, poor and discontented subjects of mine join them. They rob and steal, and even threaten to overrun the whole country, and turn me and the royal household out. I have had a council of war with my ministers and advisers, and all of us agree there is only one man who can put an end to this terrible danger. And that is you, the giant-killer, husband of my only daughter, and hero of all the people. You will not refuse me, I know.'

What could poor Johnny do? It was useless to say that he had given up giant-killing and settled down to be a quiet family man. The country was in danger. He could not refuse. So he told the King that he would do what he could. Then he sat down and thought about the rebellion, and the more he thought about it, the less he liked it.

However, early next morning he rose up, buckled on his old sword, and kissed the Princess fondly. She wished him good luck, and he went off to the King's palace, where the King had promised to give him a horse to take him to the rebels' camp. In the courtyard of the palace three strong men were trying to hold a great black charger with prancing hooves and snorting nostrils.

'There!' said the King with pride. 'Isn't he a beauty? Did you ever see such a horse?'

'No,' said Johnny. 'Is that for me?'

'Why, yes,' said the King. 'That's the only steed in the kingdom worthy of a hero like yourself.'

Johnny thought he would rather walk, but he only said:

'I'm not a very good rider, Your Majesty. Perhaps a *smaller* horse would do just as well.'

'Nonsense!' said the King. 'You won't need to ride him; just hold on, and he'll fly away with you.'

That's just what I'm afraid of, thought Johnny, but he did not say so. Just then, one of the three men who were trying to hold the horse was kicked over backwards.

'He's getting a little restless,' said the King. 'Perhaps you ought to be starting.'

'Perhaps I ought,' said Johnny, and one of the men helped him up into the saddle.

The other man threw him the reins, and Johnny was about to turn and wave to the King when he saw that the King was no longer there. Or rather, Johnny was no longer there, for the black horse had shot out of the palace gate like a cannon-ball. All he could do was to hang on. As he thundered through the streets, the people waved and cheered, and mothers held their frightened children to their skirts for fear they might be trampled by the four great hooves.

In three minutes, Johnny was out of the town and in the open country. On and on he thundered, mile after mile.

'Now that's a wonderful rider!' said an old farmer who was hoeing a field by the roadside. ''Tis a marvel how he manages to stay in the saddle—that it is.'

26

This is exactly what Johnny himself was thinking at that moment; but stay in the saddle he did, somehow, and before long he reached the country of the rebels.

Now it happened that, at the top of a hill, a gallows had been set up at a crossroads long ago. It had been used to hang thieves on, but it was old and rotten. Any day a strong wind might blow it over. And as Johnny approached on the black horse, that is just what happened. There was a gust of wind over the hilltop, and the old gallows fell down right on the horse's neck, and there it stuck fast. If Johnny had known how, he would have pulled up the horse and taken the gallows off. But this he could not do, and on they rode, faster and faster down the hill with the gallows firmly stuck on the horse's neck for all to see. With one hand Johnny held on firmly to the horse's mane, and with the other he brandished the rusty sword. And this is how the rebels first saw him as they stood round their camp at the bottom of the hill.

They were quite unprepared for any attack, and the first warning they had was the terrible thundering of the horse's hooves. There was no time to run for their weapons. The first man to sight Johnny shouted in terror:

'Mercy on us! Here's Johnny Gloke, the great giant-killer, come with a gallows to hang us all!'

'Him that killed the two giants single-handed?' cried another.

'It's Johnny Gloke,' cried a third, 'come to kill us all! It's Gloke the giant-killer with an army behind him!'

So the word went through the rebels' camp, and they all fled for their lives. The rebel leader tried to make some stay and fight, but they refused to, for the word had got round that

Johnny had gathered an army and was coming to string them all up on a row of gibbets.

Well, that was the end of the rebellion. Some of the brigands took to the hills and woods, and some returned home. But the country was left in peace, and there was no more robbing and raiding. The King was overcome with gratitude, and Johnny was more popular than ever. His fame rose even higher, and he became the greatest hero the country had ever known. After this, he was allowed to live in peace in his own castle with his admiring wife, the golden-haired Princess. And in time to come, when the King died, Johnny became King after him, and never had there been such a time of peace, plenty, and good fortune.

THE FISH AND THE RING

❖

In the county of Yorkshire, in the north part of England, there lived a baron. He had a fine castle and many rich and noble friends. All day he hunted or rode over his estate; but at night, when everyone else had gone to bed, and all was quiet, he sat up late and studied strange books; for he was a magician. Hour after hour, by the light of a lamp, he would sit over some great leather-bound book trying to discover, by signs and calculations, everything that was going to happen in the world.

He had one son, a boy of five years old; and him he loved more than all others; for the boy's mother had died, and the Baron had only his son to love. Of course he wanted him to be happy and get on in the world. He hoped he would grow up and marry some wealthy lady, perhaps a princess, and have a splendid palace and rule over a great kingdom. So he determined to find out who it was his son was going to marry.

All night he worked and worked at his books, and at last, when it was nearly morning, he knew the answer; and the Baron was sad at heart: for instead of a rich princess, he discovered that his son would grow up and marry the daughter of a very poor, humble man who lived under the shadow of the Minster in the city of York. The Baron had worked at his magic for hours, trying to find a mistake in his calculations; but to no purpose. There could be no possible mistake.

It was no use the Baron going to bed; he could not sleep. Nor could he eat any breakfast. Instead, he hurried down the winding stairs and out into the great courtyard. Not a soul was stirring. He saddled a horse and rode off towards the city of York.

When the Baron came to the great Minster, he noticed a poor old man outside the door of the cottage. He looked so miserable that the Baron asked him what was wrong.

'Sir,' said the poor man, 'I have five young children, and now my wife has had a baby girl, and I do not know where the money is to come from to feed and clothe them all. We are very poor, and I fear I cannot work hard enough.'

Ah, thought the Baron, this is indeed the girl who is to grow up and marry my son. Never shall he be wed to the child of such a wretched soul living in this miserable hovel.

So he pretended to be kind and charitable and smiled at the old man.

'Old man,' said the Baron, 'I will do you a kindness. Give me the child, and I will take her to my home and she shall be well looked after.'

The old man and his wife did not want to lose their daughter, but they thought it would be the best thing for her in the end. It was not a chance to be missed. So amid tears and farewells, they gave the baby girl to the Baron, and he rode away as quickly as he could from the city of York.

Over the moors he rode until he came to a broad valley

with a river winding through it. Feeling bitter and angry at heart, he got off his horse, took the baby to the river, and dropped her in.

'Never shall fate cause my boy, my only son, to wed the daughter of a wretched poor fellow. He shall have a better wife than that.'

So, muttering to himself, he leapt once more on to his horse and rode away, not stopping till he came to his own castle.

But fate was kind to the helpless baby. No sooner had she fallen into the water than her baby-clothes spread out and she floated gently down the stream. She did not even feel wet or cold, for she was peacefully asleep.

Now, a little farther downstream sat a poor man who lived in a cottage not far away. He was trying to catch fish. He had sat there all the morning, but never a fish had come to bite at his line. He was just thinking of giving up and going home when he caught sight of the tiny girl floating on the water towards him.

'Well,' said he to himself, 'this is an odder fish than ever I saw before. Come away, my little one, and let's see what thou art.'

So he pulled the baby gently towards him with his fishing-rod and lifted her out of the water. He took off her wet clothes, wrapped her up in his own dry shawl, and made off home as fast as he could, for fear the child had caught cold.

But the girl grew strong and healthy under the care of the fisherman and his wife. They had her christened Margaret and looked after her as if she had been their own. She grew into a gay and happy child, and most beautiful besides. It would be pleasant to tell of her life with the fisherman and his wife in their cottage on the moors, but we must get on with the story.

2

Sixteen years passed, and now the Baron's only son had grown into a fine young man of twenty-one. He was a restless fellow, and did not always like to stay with his father in the castle. Instead, he would roam the country and sometimes spend weeks or months at a time with his uncle at Scarborough, on the sea-coast. His father wondered sometimes when the young man would choose himself a wife, but he knew it was no use worrying. Besides, he grew more and more interested in his magic, and read still more and more strange and wonderful books. So that he did not always know where his son was for weeks at a time.

One day, the Baron was out riding with some of his followers, and they lost their way on the moors. It was a hot day, and they could find no water. Presently they reached the fisherman's cottage, where they saw Margaret sitting at the door getting vegetables ready for her foster-parents' dinner.

They got off their horses, and the Baron asked the girl if she could bring them some water. Margaret, who had now grown into a beautiful young woman, got up, wiped her hands on her apron, and did as she was asked. The fisherman and his wife came out, and they and the girl and the Baron and his followers all talked together in a friendly way, while the men refreshed themselves with cool water and new scones.

'That is a very beautiful girl,' said one of the Baron's friends. 'It would be an interesting matter to know whom she will marry. Are you promised to anyone?' he asked her.

'No, sir,' said Margaret. 'We are poor folk, and I have to help my parents. We have no time to think of weddings and such-like. Besides, there is no one round here who would want to wed a poor girl like me.'

'Well, if I had a son of my own,' said the nobleman, 'I would want no fairer wife for him than this.'

'You are a learned man,' said another nobleman to the Baron, 'and can read mysteries and tell fortunes. What sort of man is this sweet girl likely to marry?'

Suddenly the Baron was afraid.

'I am no gypsy,' he said. 'Ask me to tell no fortunes.'

But his followers pressed him, telling him his magic was all a pretence, and he could no more guess the future than they could. So at last the Baron gave in, and said he would try to find out what kind of man the girl was going to wed. He asked the fisherman's wife when her daughter was born, for that was the first thing he had to know.

'Truth to tell, sir,' said the woman, 'this is not our daughter. We found her just sixteen years ago to this day.'

'Yes, indeed,' said her husband. 'It was I that found our poor Margaret floating on the river not many miles from this very cottage.'

'Which river is that?' asked the Baron. No one noticed that he had turned very pale and was speaking more quietly than usual. The fisherman told him the name of the river.

'How old was she then, would you say?' asked the Baron.

'Not more than a few days,' answered the fisherman's wife.

The Baron said nothing, for he knew this was the girl whom fate had intended to marry his son. He had tried to drown her sixteen years ago, but here she was alive and grown-up. The woman went inside the cottage and came out with a long grey shawl.

'This is the very shawl my man found her in,' she said. 'I can't tell where she came from, but this is a pattern that mothers used to knit for their babies in the city of York. I know, for my sister used to live there in bygone days.'

The Baron asked one of his followers for paper and ink. Then he sat down on the bench outside the cottage and wrote a letter. This he sealed up and gave to Margaret.

'Here,' said he, 'I like you, and I will make your fortune. Take this letter to my brother in Scarborough, and he will look after you. Here is money to see you on your way. Good luck go with you—and may you come back to your parents safe and sound, when your fortune is made.'

Margaret and her foster-parents were so surprised at this offer that they hardly knew what to say. But they thanked the Baron, and soon he rode off with his nobles.

Next day, Margaret set off to find the Baron's brother in Scarborough, with the letter tucked safely into her skirt. Away she tramped through the fields and over the moors, but she was still a fair distance from Scarborough when evening came on. So she decided to stay the night at an inn. She found a decent, comfortable inn at a village, and there she had a meal and settled down for the night.

Now at that inn there happened to be two robbers. They were on the lookout for rich travellers who might be passing that way. Having nothing better to do, they waited until Margaret was asleep and stole into her room. They looked through her possessions and found the Baron's letter to his brother. Going to their room, they read the letter by the light of a candle. This is what it said:

'My dear Brother,
Seize hold of the bearer of this letter and put her to death instantly. She will otherwise prove a danger to our family.
Your loving brother,
John.'

The two robbers were most indignant at this, and took pity on the poor girl.

'What a shame,' they said, 'to murder such an innocent creature.'

So they took pen and ink and wrote another letter, sealed it up, and put it in Margaret's pocket instead of the first letter. And all the time Margaret was asleep and had no idea of what was going on.

Next morning she rose up early, paid for her night's lodging and set out for Scarborough. By noon she had arrived at the town and soon found her way to the home of the Baron's brother.

It so happened that the Baron's son, now twenty-one years old, was staying there; on seeing the beautiful girl come into the courtyard, he asked her what her business was; and on being told, he led her to his uncle.

Margaret gave him the letter. He unsealed it—and this is what it said:

'My dear Brother,
Take the girl who brings this letter and

marry her to my son. She is a sweet maid and
needs your protection.
                        Your loving brother,
                                John.'

Well, the Baron's brother was a little surprised at this letter, but he knew his brother was a strange man; he was also a
little afraid of him, seeing that he was a powerful magician.
So, seeing that his young nephew was enchanted with the
beauty of the girl, he made preparations for the wedding.
Margaret and the Baron's son spent several happy days walking and talking by the sea and in the woods outside the town.

Back in his castle, the Baron was amazed to receive a letter from his brother in Scarborough saying that he had done
as the Baron wished and made arrangements for the instant
marriage of his son to the beautiful girl who had brought his
letter.

He turned very pale as he saw that there had been a mistake. Once again he had his horse saddled and rode off
instantly to his brother's house. When he arrived in the courtyard, he saw that there were indeed preparations for a wedding. Men were carrying in great joints of meat and baskets of
provisions, and others were wheeling barrels of wine towards
the house. The sound of music could be heard coming from
the windows of the hall. He threw his reins to an ostler and
strode angrily into the house.

'Where is the girl who is to many my son?' he called.

At the sight of Margaret in her wedding-dress, his anger
rose, but he calmed himself. He told his brother that he must
talk with Margaret before the ceremony could begin; then he

led the girl out of the house, across the courtyard and through the streets until he came to the cliffs outside the town.

Once more, the Baron had determined to interfere with the fate that had destined this girl to be the wife of his only son. Poor Margaret could not understand what was happening. Then she saw that he was leading her towards the edge of the cliff, and knew what he was about to do.

She went down on her knees and begged him not to kill her.

'Only let me go,' she pleaded, 'and I will never set eyes on you or your son again. I have done nothing to harm anyone. Please do not harm me. I will go away and never be seen again in your country.'

So pitifully did she plead that the Baron grew calm and decided to have mercy on her. He noticed upon her finger a ring that had once belonged to him. His son must have given it to her. He drew it off her finger and flung it far out to sea. It gleamed for a second before it sank into the water.

'Girl,' said the Baron, 'I will let you go. Let that be an end to your marriage with my son. If ever I see you again I shall put you to death as I tried to once before. But,' he added, 'if ever you can show me that ring again, you shall have the hand of my son in marriage, and my blessing into the bargain!'

Then he laughed and turned away, leaving the sobbing girl to look after herself. The Baron went back to his brother's house and told them there would be no wedding, for the bride had run away to her home, and they would never see her more. It was in vain for his brother and the young man to ask what he meant. They knew that the Baron was a violent man, and there was no reasoning with him when his mind was fixed.

3

But Margaret did not go back to the fisherman's cottage. Instead, she found work as a kitchen-maid in the castle of a wealthy nobleman in another part of the country. She had much work to do, for the nobleman was always entertaining big parties of guests. Her services were much in demand, for at the fisherman's cottage she had learnt well how to prepare meat and vegetables and fish for the table. She worked hard for several months, and presently was happy and content again, disappointed though she had been to lose the young man she had been going to marry.

One day she was busy preparing a huge fish in the castle kitchen, when who should ride up to the gate but the young man himself and his father the Baron, together with a great company of huntsmen. So this was the party for whom a banquet was being prepared! These were the people who were to sit down in the great hall and eat the meat and pastry and dishes of all kinds which she and the cooks were preparing. She determined to make a wonderful dish of the fish she was cleaning and to be especially careful to make it tasty and appetizing. She turned her eyes away from the window through which she had been looking and began to attend to the fish. Then she noticed something gleaming inside it, something small and golden and shining. She took it out, washed it in fresh water, and carried it to the window to look at it closely. It was a ring—yes, the very ring that the Baron's son had given her, the very ring that the Baron had taken off her finger and thrown into the sea near Scarborough. She put it into her pocket; and when her work was done and the great fish was cooking in one of the ovens, she washed her hands and put the ring carefully on her finger.

In the great hall, the company were delighted with the splendid dinner the nobleman had provided. There was rich food and delicious wine; the Baron was in high good humour, for he had determined on a wealthy bride for his son. It is true that his son did not care for the lady, and often thought sadly of the sweet girl he had seen at the house of his uncle; but no doubt he would obey his father's command and marry according to his choice. There was laughter and talking among the guests as the food and wine was served in great style and abundance. One dish in particular pleased the company, and that was a splendid fish that was served whole, covered in the most appetizing sauce imaginable and garnished with herbs. Never had they tasted such a fish! The Baron determined on having the cook sent for, that he might compliment her on her art. So, very shyly, yet confidently and calmly, Margaret was led down the hall to where the Baron was sitting. At first he did not recognize her. Then, as all the guests fell silent to see such a charming, modest, and beautiful girl in the humble apron of a kitchen-maid, he looked into her face and knew who she was. He was too amazed to be angry. How could he be angry with such a girl in front of the admiring company!

'Your cooking,' he said quietly, 'is unrivalled. It could not be better if it were done by magic.'

She had curtsied low beside his chair. He took her by the hand and slowly raised her up. As he did so, he saw that on the hand he held there was a ring.

'I am glad to see you, sir,' she said, 'for I have something belonging to you, and I would like to return it.'

She took off the ring and gave it him. He knew, almost without looking at it, what ring it was. Then he saw that it was no use trying to interfere with fate for a third time. He remembered his promise to her on the cliffs near Scarborough.

'You have given me back what was mine,' he said. 'If you still wish it, I will give you back what was always meant to be yours.'

Then the nobleman, who was standing near them, spoke.

'It seems,' said he, 'that you are well pleased with my little cook. I trust you will not try to take her from me.'

'She is no cook,' said the Baron in clear, bold tones. 'She is no cook, but the destined wife of my only son. Whom fate has joined, no man shall keep apart!'

And with these words he called his son to him and gave him the girl. For a long time Margaret and the young man stood gazing in happiness and amazement at one another, while the guests marvelled at this strange adventure.

So, amid great rejoicing, the two were betrothed, and not long afterwards a great and solemn wedding was held at the Baron's castle. Ever afterwards, he himself was the loudest in Margaret's praise, and the first to admit that nowhere could a better wife have been found for his son.

THE TWO PRINCESSES

———— ❖ ————

There was once a king who had one daughter and she
was called Ann. Her eyes were dark, and her hair was
long and golden, and people used to like looking upon
her. When Ann was fourteen, her mother died. When two
years had passed, the King married for a second time. His wife
also had a daughter, and her name was Kate. Kate's eyes were
not beautiful, but they were merry; her hair was short and of
a middling brown colour. She was pleasant and kind and good.
Soon the two girls were fast friends. They loved each other,
and spent all their time together; walking in the meadows,
reading the same books, and enjoying everything that went on
about the King's castle.

But the new queen was a jealous woman. She saw that her
stepdaughter Ann was beautiful, while her own daughter was
not. Kate was pleasant enough to look at, and by herself she
might be thought beautiful. But when she was with Ann, as
usually she was, people did not look at her as they looked at
Ann. So the Queen began to hate her stepdaughter and try to
think of some way in which she could spoil her beauty.

One day, as she was walking in her apartments, biting her

nails in restless spite, she thought of the old hen-wife who lived near the castle gate. This was an old woman who lived in a tiny cottage and looked after the hens who laid the eggs that were sent to the castle kitchen.

'I will go and talk to the hen-wife,' said the Queen to herself. 'She is a clever woman and is thought to have magical powers.'

Now the Queen had never been to the hen-wife's cottage before, but she knew the way; so wrapping her cloak about her, she set out and was soon knocking at the old woman's door.

'Old woman,' she said as soon as she was inside, 'they tell me you can do marvellous things, but I don't believe them. My stepdaughter is far more beautiful than is good for her, and is becoming proud and vain. So far, you have only been paid for your eggs in silver; but if you can tell me a way of spoiling my stepdaughter's beauty just a little, to teach her a lesson, I will pay for every egg that you send with a piece of gold.'

'Nothing could be simpler,' said the old hen-wife. 'Call that a task? Why, that's hardly worth my troubling about. Send the Princess to me in the morning, and you shall see what I can do.'

'Very well,' answered the Queen. 'The Princess will be here first thing in the morning.'

'Only,' said the hen-wife, 'you must remember one thing. Not a bite must she eat and not a drop must she drink before she comes; otherwise I can do nothing.'

'Not a drop will she drink, not a bite will she eat,' said the Queen. 'I will not forget.'

So saying, she was gone.

Next morning the Queen stopped her stepdaughter as she was on her way to breakfast.

'Good morning, child,' she said. 'You are looking pale, and a little air before breakfast will give you an appetite. For breakfast you shall have a new-laid egg, or perhaps two if you go and fetch them quickly. Run down to the hen-wife's cottage at once and ask her for some eggs.'

So Ann ran off towards the cottage; but on the way she went through the castle kitchen, and there she saw a crust of bread lying on the table. So, being hungry, for she had had no breakfast, she snatched up the crust and ran with it to the castle gate, eating it as she went.

Presently she reached the old woman's tiny cottage with its one chimney smoking straight up into the morning sky. She knocked on the door, and the old woman let her in.

'You are early, my dear,' said the hen-wife. 'What do you want?'

'If you please,' said Ann. 'I have come for some new-laid eggs.'

'Well, just step over there, lift the lid of that pot, and see what you find inside.'

The cottage was dark, and Ann did not notice that the hen-wife had a cunning smile on her pinched and wrinkled face. She went across to the cooking-stove, on which was standing a round, black pot with a lid on. She lifted the lid and looked in.

But nothing happened.

The hen-wife's cunning smile vanished, but she did not show her annoyance.

43

'Go home, my dear,' she said, 'and tell your stepmother to keep the larder locked in future.'

Ann thought this was a strange message, but she did not stop any longer, and went back to the castle.

Next day, the Queen decided to try again.

'Daughter,' she said, 'you are looking pale, and the morning air will do you good. Go down to the hen-wife's cottage and ask her for some new-laid eggs.'

Off went Ann once more. This time there was no crust on the kitchen-table; but, passing through a field where men were working, she noticed that they were gathering peas. She talked pleasantly to the men, and they gave her a handful of the peas. She was glad enough to eat them on her way, for she had had no breakfast, and the morning air was fresh. Presently she came to the hen-wife's cottage. Once more she asked for eggs.

'Just step over there, my dear,' said the old woman, 'look inside that pot, and see what you can find.'

Ann did as she was told. She lifted the lid of the round black pot, and once again nothing happened.

'Go home,' said the hen-wife, 'and tell the Queen that the pot won't boil if the fire's away.'

Ann went back to the castle and told her stepmother what the old woman had said.

The Queen at once understood by this that Ann must once again have found something to eat on the way to the old woman's cottage, even though she had gone there before breakfast. This time she determined to go with her and see that she had nothing to eat.

So, next morning the Queen and the Princess set off

together. Ann had had nothing to eat since she got up. When they reached the cottage and asked for more new-laid eggs, once again the hen-wife told Ann to look in the pot. She did so, and this time out popped a sheep's head and fastened itself on Ann's shoulders instead of her own.

'There,' said the old woman gleefully, 'she won't be quite so proud of her pretty face now.'

'No,' said the Queen, 'people won't look at her in quite the way they used to, will they? Perhaps they'll look a little more kindly at my Kate from now on. I must admit you were as good as your word, old woman. Here are the golden guineas I promised you.'

She handed a purse to the hen-wife and set out with her stepdaughter to the castle.

When they got there, everyone was horror-struck to see what had happened to Ann. Gone were her lovely gold tresses, her dark eyes, and rosy cheeks—instead, how silly she looked with her grey sheep's face surrounded by woolly fleeces.

When Kate saw her stepsister, she burst out crying.

'Oh, my pretty dear,' she said, 'what has happened?'

Nobody knew, of course, except for the Queen, and she said nothing. Poor Ann could only make baa-ing noises like a sheep.

'We must get help,' said Kate to herself. 'This will never do. Somewhere there must be someone able to give my sister back her own face and her lovely hair.'

So when there was no one in sight, she covered Ann's head in a thick white shawl, put on her own cloak and bonnet, and set off with Ann into the wide world.

At last, when the two sisters were almost worn out with weariness and night was coming on, they reached another castle. They knocked at the gate and were soon let in. Presently a lady-in-waiting came to see what they wanted. Kate told her they had lost their way and wanted shelter for the night.

'I don't know whether you can stop here,' said the lady-in-waiting. 'Everyone is very worried, for one of the Princes has been sick for a long time, and no one can cure him.'

'My sister is sick too,' said Kate. 'Oh, please let us in. We will do no one any harm.'

Well, the lady-in-waiting was sorry for the Princesses, and she liked the way Kate spoke and looked. So she went to see the sick Prince's father and mother, who were King and Queen in that part of the country.

Presently she returned.

'Well,' she said, 'I have talked to Their Majesties, and you may stop in the castle on one condition.'

'Oh, anything,' said Kate eagerly. 'I will do anything if only my poor sister and I can stay.'

So the lady-in-waiting told Kate that she must sit up and nurse the sick Prince whom no one could cure.

'If you do this,' she added, 'you may stay the night, and you will be given a purse full of silver for your trouble. But there is one difficulty which I must tell you of. Many have sat up at night to nurse the Prince, but in the middle of the night each one has disappeared. You run a great risk. Will you do it?'

'Oh yes,' said Kate without hesitation. 'I am sure nothing will happen to me.'

So it was agreed. Kate took her sister upstairs to the room

where the Prince lay ill. She and Ann were brought food and drink, and the lady-in-waiting left them for the night.

All was quiet until the great bell in the castle tower sounded the strokes of midnight. Then the Prince got up, put on his clothes, and went softly downstairs. Kate left her sister asleep in a corner near the fire and followed the Prince. He fetched his horse from the stable and called to his hound. Then he jumped up on the horse, and Kate jumped up behind him. With the hound leading the way, they rode out of the castle yard. On and on they rode through the moonlit country, till they presently entered a thick wood. As they brushed past the trees and bushes, Kate put out her hand and gathered ripe nuts, with which she filled her pockets. Presently they left the wood and approached a steep green hillside. Here the hound stopped and sniffed the ground, and the Prince reined in his horse.

'Open, open, green hill,' cried he, 'and let in the young Prince with his horse and his hound!'

A door in the hillside opened and the Prince rode in. There was a sound of music and merriment from a great lighted hall. It was the hall of the fairies, and a magnificent ball was in progress. The Prince got down from his horse. Kate jumped off too and hid herself behind the door to watch what went on. No one noticed her.

Gaily and happily the Prince danced, first with one fairy and then another, stepping in stately manner down the long hall or whirling madly round between the great columns, while the fairy band played in their sweetest and gayest tones.

So the hours passed. Then all at once the cock crew, and the Prince left off dancing and called for his horse. He leapt into the saddle, and Kate leapt up behind him; then the hound led them out of the hall under the hall, and they were once more galloping back towards the castle.

In the morning, when the castle servants came in to draw the curtains, make up the fire, and bring breakfast, they found Kate sitting beside the fireplace cracking nuts and the Prince sleeping peacefully in bed.

'Has he had a good night?' they asked.

'He has had a very good night,' answered Kate. She was given her purse full of silver and asked if she would sit up and watch for a second night.

'Yes, indeed,' she answered, 'but this time I must have a peck of gold.'

This was agreed to, and that night Kate and her sister stayed with the Prince as before.

And when the great clock sounded midnight, once more the Prince rose up and went downstairs and brought out his horse and his hound, and mounted the horse with Kate behind him. Once more they sped through the lanes and fields, and once more Kate plucked nuts in the thick wood and stuffed them in her pockets.

They came again to the green hill, and the Prince called out: 'Open, open, green hill, and let in the young Prince and his horse and his hound.'

Once more the hillside opened and the Prince rode in. It was just the same as before, only, if anything, the music was sweeter and gayer and the lights brighter and the dancers more lively and nimble. Kate hid herself behind the door and watched. How beautiful the fairies were with their long dresses of floating silver and gold cloth, rose-coloured silk, white satin, and embroidered gauze! And how handsome and gallant were the tall cavaliers who steered them through the mazes of the dance! Once more, the Prince grew weary with the mad dancing, though he looked happy and carefree.

Kate looked down and noticed that a baby fairy was playing near her feet with a silver wand. And she overheard two fairies talking close by. One of them said:

'One touch of that wand would cure the Princess's sick sister.'

Kate said nothing, but as soon as the fairies were not looking she began to roll some of her nuts towards the baby fairy. The baby laughed with delight, and put out her hands to catch the nuts. Presently she had forgotten all about the silver wand, for silver wands are much commoner toys to fairy babies than they are to human children. Kate picked up the wand and hid it beneath her cloak.

Soon afterwards the cock crew, and the Prince jumped on his horse with Kate behind him, and off they rode through the fading moonlight. And when the castle servants came as usual in the morning to the Prince's room, there was the Prince asleep in bed and Kate sitting at the fireside cracking nuts.

'Has the Prince had a good night?' they asked.

'A very good night,' Kate answered.

When Ann awoke, Kate took away the shawl that covered her woolly sheep's head, and touched her lightly with the silver wand that she had brought from the hall under the hill. Instantly the sheep's head vanished, and there was Ann once more, just as she had been before her cruel stepmother had sent her to the hen-wife's cottage. There were her own dark eyes, her smooth cheeks, and her long, golden hair.

'Oh, Kate,' she said, 'I feel as if I had had a dream.'

'Do you?' said Kate. 'Well, perhaps you have. Now let us

have some breakfast, for you must be hungry. As for me—well, I am so hungry I feel as if I could eat a sheep's head!'

Everyone was delighted when Kate told them that her sick sister was cured; and Ann went off to talk to the castle ladies and the Prince's brothers and sisters. But Their Majesties were sad that their eldest son was still sick, and they asked Kate if she would stay yet another night. After all, the Prince was no worse, and Kate had not disappeared in the night, as all the other nurses had done, so perhaps she would be able to cure him in the end. So they gave Kate her purse full of gold and asked her to sit up another night.

'Why, yes, I will,' said Kate, 'only this time, if I do not disappear, you must let me marry the Prince; for you know,' she added, 'I am a Princess myself, and well worthy of such a husband.'

So the Prince's father promised Kate she should marry the Prince if she could cure him.

'After all,' he said to the Queen, 'if she can nurse him and cure him when no one else can, I daresay she'll make him the best wife too.'

So it was agreed, and once more Kate stayed and watched over the sleeping Prince.

For the third time, the same thing happened. At midnight, when all the castle was asleep, the Prince got up, dressed, mounted his horse with Kate behind him, and galloped off towards the green hill. For the third time, when the hound led them along the narrow track through the wood, Kate gathered nuts to eat in the morning.

'Open, open, green hill, and let in the young Prince and his horse and his hound!'

For the third time Kate heard the words of the Prince. The fairies' hall was as bright and splendid as ever, and the Prince danced gaily and happily with all the fairies who came and crowded round him. And Kate in her corner behind the door watched. As the evening wore on, she noticed a second fairy baby playing with a bird; and she overheard one fairy saying to another:

'Three bites of that bird would cure the sick Prince.'

So this time Kate rolled all her nuts for the baby to play with, and in a few minutes it had grown tired of playing with the bird and was only interested in rolling the nuts about and trying to crack them between its gums. Quickly Kate took up the bird and put it carefully in the pocket of her cloak.

At cockcrow, they set off once more for the castle, and at dawn the Prince was asleep as usual, but Kate was not cracking nuts this time, for she had given them all to the fairy baby—besides, she had something more important to do. As soon as she reached the castle, she had killed and plucked the bird, and was now cooking it in a pot over the fire. A delicious smell began to rise and fill the air; and at that the Prince awoke and asked what it came from.

Kate told him.

'Ah,' said the Prince, 'if only I could have just one bite of that bird.'

She gave him a bite, and he rose up on one elbow.

'I feel better,' said he. 'Now if I could have just one more bite from that bird—'

So Kate gave him a second bite, and this time he sat up and leant against the pillows.

51

'I feel better still,' he said. 'Oh, if I could have just one bite more—'

So Kate gave him a third bite; and at this he was completely cured and as well as ever he was. He got out of bed and put on his clothes. When the servants came in as usual, he was sitting beside Kate in front of the fire, and they had finished off the bird together and were chatting and laughing happily.

Everyone was delighted to see the Prince quite well again. All said how clever and kind Kate had been and what a good wife she would make for the Prince. And of course the Prince agreed. So preparations were made for the wedding. Meanwhile, the Prince's younger brother had seen Ann, and had instantly fallen in love with her, as everyone did who saw her. So it was agreed that they, too, should be married; a wonderful banquet was held, and all the noble men and women of the country were invited. And the sick Prince married the Princess who was well, and the sick Princess married the sick Prince's brother. The sick Prince and Princess were ill no more, nor did Kate and the Prince ever visit the fairies' hall under the hill. Instead, they lived happily ever afterwards; but the dancing went on as before under the hill, and the fairy babies grew up and never wondered what had become of the wand and the little bird. But whom they danced with when they grew up, and what coloured dresses they wore, and whether the music was as tuneful as ever—that I cannot tell.

THE STORY OF TOM THUMB

❖

I n the days of King Arthur, there lived a famous magician called Merlin. One day, when he was travelling the country disguised as a beggar, he stopped at the cottage of a poor ploughman to ask for food. The ploughman had just come in from work, and was sitting down to supper. He was very tired, but he welcomed the stranger, even though this was only a ragged beggar man; and the ploughman's wife said he could sit down and share their supper.

Now Merlin noticed that the ploughman and his wife, though they had a snug cottage and enough to eat, did not seem happy.

'What is the matter?' he asked. 'What is it you lack?'

'Why,' said the ploughman's wife, 'my husband and I have lived here happily enough for nearly twenty years, but we have no child. This is a great sorrow to us. How I should love to have had a son—yes, even a little son no bigger than my husband's thumb. However small he was, I should not mind, just so as I could call him my own and look after him.'

Well, the beggar said nothing, and soon afterwards took his leave. But thinking over what the poor woman had said,

Merlin said to himself, 'What a good idea to give this woman just what she wants.' So by magic he brought it about that the ploughman's wife had a little boy no bigger than the plough-man's thumb. They loved him dearly and named him Tom Thumb, and he never grew an inch bigger, but was always just the same size as his father's thumb.

One moonlight night, the Fairy Queen happened to look in at the window of the cottage. She flew inside and kissed Tom, and ordered her fairies to make him a suit of clothes. They made him a shirt of spider's web, a jacket of thistle-down, trousers of feathers, stockings of apple peel, and a little pair of shoes of mouse-skin, with the fur on the inside. Then on top of his head was placed an oak-leaf cap; and these were the clothes that Tom wore, winter and summer, greatly to the admiration of his mother and all the neighbours round about.

As he grew older, Tom was full of tricks. He used to play at cherry-stones with the boys from the village. When he had no stone of his own, he would creep into the bags belonging to the boys and steal their stones. One sharp-eyed lad caught sight of him doing this, and just as Tom had got his head inside the boy's bag, he pulled the string tight and made Tom howl with pain.

'That'll serve you right for stealing!' said the boy with the bag.

'I'll never steal again!' cried Tom. 'Only let me out, and I'll never steal again!'

So Tom was let out; and—for a time at least—he stole no more cherry-stones.

Tom was so small that, although his mother loved him dearly, she sometimes lost sight of him, especially when she was busy. One day she was making a batter pudding and chanced to leave the kitchen for a moment. Tom climbed on to the edge of the basin to see what was inside; his foot slipped, and splash! he fell right into the batter. His mother poured the mixture into the pan and began cooking it. Tom's mouth was so full of the pudding that he could not call out, but he kicked and struggled for all he was worth.

'Well, now,' said Tom's mother, 'I do declare that pudding is bewitched. An evil spirit has got into it, and it's good for nothing.'

So she tipped the pudding out of the window. Just then a tinker happened to be passing, and being hungry, he thought the pudding would do for his dinner. So he picked it up and put it in his wallet. But by this time Tom had got his mouth free of the batter and began to holler out loud.

'Oh, my!' said the tinker. 'Now what's got into my bag, I wonder? 'Tis some evil spirit come to frighten me for picking up that pudding.'

So without looking into his wallet, he opened it as quickly as he could and tipped everything out, Tom and pudding and all. Shaking the rest of the batter from his clothes and picking up his oak-leaf cap, which had fallen off, Tom ran home as fast as he could. His mother was overjoyed at seeing him again, gave him a good wash in a teacup full of warm water, kissed him, and put him to bed.

Next day, his mother took him out to the field with her when she went to milk the cow. It was a windy day, and she was afraid the little boy would get blown away. So while she did her milking, she tied him to a thistle. But the cow, seeing only his oak-leaf cap, thought she would like a tasty mouthful, so she gobbled up the thistle and Tom as well. Inside the cow's mouth, Tom was terrified of the two great rows of teeth, so he called out with all his might:

'Mother, Mother! Help, help!'

'Where are you?' cried his mother, getting up from her milking-stool and looking round for the thistle where she had tied her son for safety.

'Here!' called Tom. 'Inside the cow's mouth!'

But the cow was so surprised to hear a shrill voice coming from inside her own mouth that she opened her jaws and let Tom fall. As luck would have it, his mother held out her apron and caught Tom just in time.

Tom's next adventure happened when he was out in the fields driving the cattle along with a whip which his father had made him of a barley straw. He slipped on some rough ground and fell into a furrow. Before he could pick himself up, a great black raven flew down and carried him off in her beak. Away she flew, over hills and valleys, until she came to the sea—and there she dropped him.

Down and down fell Tom Thumb, till at last he struck the water. Then snap!—a great fish with wide-open jaws swallowed him up in a moment and carried him out to sea. But a fishing-boat caught up the fish in its nets, and next day this very fish, with Tom inside, was brought to the court of King Arthur himself. When the cook cut open the fish to prepare it for the King's dinner, how surprised she was to find Tom inside! Alive and well he was, though a little frightened at his adventure; and all the scullions and the kitchen-maids gathered round to look at him. Then the cook took him up to the King himself; and there stood Tom, on the King's own table, bowing and taking off his oak-leaf hat to all the ladies and the knights of the Round Table. Everyone laughed and clapped hands, and Tom was made the King's dwarf and became a great favourite. They all wondered where he had come from. Only Merlin, the magician, could tell, but he said nothing.

'Tell me what your parents are like,' said the King to Tom one day. 'Are they little folk, just like yourself?'

'Why, no,' said Tom, 'my father and mother are poor labouring folk, just like those who work in your fields. They are no bigger and no smaller than others are; but perhaps they are poorer than most.'

'Well,' said the King, who was very fond of Tom, 'go into my treasury, where I keep all my money, and take as much gold or silver as you can carry. Go home with it, and give it to your poor father and mother.'

So Tom went to King Arthur's treasury with a bag made from a water bubble. But all he could get into the bag was a silver threepenny piece, and even this was almost too heavy for him. Away he trudged with his load on his back, and it took him two days and two nights to reach home. His mother and father were delighted to see him, and they cooked a fine meal and made much of him, for he was nearly dead with weariness after carrying the silver piece so far. They were proud to have the silver piece, especially when they knew it was a present from King Arthur himself; and many an evening he spent telling them of his adventures at court and what a great favourite he was with all the lords and ladies.

After a few weeks, he kissed them goodbye and went back to the King's castle, for he was afraid the King would be missing his dwarf; and very pleased they all were at court to see him again. There is no time to tell all the adventures that befell him after that; but we will finish by describing how King Arthur made him one of his knights.

First he must have a new suit, for his other clothes, that he had had from the Fairy Queen, had become torn and ragged from his adventures in the batter pudding and the cow's mouth and the great fish. So the court tailors were ordered to make him a new coat of butterflies' wings, and the royal boot-maker made him a pair of boots of chicken hide. Then he was knighted before the assembled court and given a needle for a sword and a sleek white mouse for a horse. And on fine days he would go hunting with all the courtiers, his sword by his side, and his mouse steed trotting beneath him.

The King also had a chair of state made for him so that he might sit on the royal table and amuse the Queen at meal times; and a little gold palace was made for him to live in with a great door an inch wide. But for all his finery, Sir Thomas Thumb, as he was now called, never forgot his humble parents. Once a month, he rode off on his white mouse to their cottage in the country and amused the old folks with tales and talk from the court of King Arthur. So that the poor ploughman and his wife had good cause to be proud of the little son they had been given through the magic of the great Merlin, whom they had entertained unknown, years ago, in the form of an old and tattered beggar.

THE PEDLAR'S DREAM

❖

There was once a poor pedlar named John, who lived in the village of Swaffham in Norfolk. He kept himself and his wife and three children as best he could in their small cottage, but they were always poor, for John was not much of a tradesman. He was too simple for this world, and too honest to make as much money as he might have done out of the poor folks who came to buy his wares at fairs and markets. Day after day he would tramp the roads with his pack on his back, selling pins and laces, ribbons and handkerchiefs to whoever would buy them, and singing songs and ballads at the country fairs.

One year it happened that spring came late, and when it came it was unusually wet and windy; so that poor John could not get out on the roads as much as he wanted. It was an anxious time for him and his wife, and it was with difficulty that they kept their three children fed and clothed. The boy wanted new boots when he went out to work on the farm, and the two girls had grown out of all their dresses and badly needed new ones.

'I don't know how we shall manage,' sighed the pedlar's

wife one wet morning, 'I really don't. You'll have to get yourself work on the farm, John, for there's no money in peddling, these days.'

'With all this wet weather,' answered the pedlar, 'there's none too much work on the farms neither. I tell you what, wife, I'm thinking of going up to London as soon as the rain clears.'

'London!' said his wife. 'And what would you do there, I wonder? Make all our fortunes, no doubt. Why, the sharp folks in London would cheat you out of your very clothes. What makes you want to go there?'

'Well,' said the pedlar, 'I tell you what it is. Last night, what with the rain on the roof, and me worrying and fretting about business, I couldn't sleep too well. I was restless, as you might say. And when I did get to sleep, I had a wonderful dream—a wonderful dream, wife.'

'I suppose you dreamed that a cupboard full of new clothes was come down the chimney, and when you woke up you found it was nothing but the old rook's nest that has been lodged there a twelvemonth.'

'No, that I didn't,' said John. 'What I dreamed was nothing but a voice, but it was a kind voice, and who it came from I don't know. But this is what it said. "John," it said, "if you was to go and stand on London Bridge, you'd hear a wonderful piece of news".'

'What news?' asked his wife.

'Ah, that it didn't say,' said John, 'for it was then I woke up. But it was a kind sort of a voice and sounded as if it meant what it said.'

'And you're thinking of going all the way to London just

because you have a dream in the night, and all because of eating stale cheese, I shouldn't wonder!'

'Now, nobody in this world ever had a dream in the night on account of *your* cooking, my dear,' said the pedlar.

'Well, it's small wonder if they don't,' said his wife, 'for it's precious little I have to cook. And what's the wonderful news you'll hear on London Bridge? I suppose you expect to hear that your old father has died and left us a fortune?'

'Well, something like that perhaps—except that my old father has no fortune to leave. 'Tis a foolish idea, no doubt, so we'll say no more about it.'

But the pedlar had another restless night, and still another. And both nights the same voice seemed to say to him, 'John, if you go and stand on London Bridge, you shall hear a wonderful piece of news'.

'It may be the voice of an angel,' said John, 'or of the Lord himself, sent to help a poor creature in his hour of need.'

Well, simple as he was, when John had an idea in his head, there was no getting it out; so in the end his wife agreed that he should go; she gave him her blessing and told him she would be more than pleased if he only came back with his life. So she made him wear his warmest clothes and gave him the rest of the little money they had, and he kissed his family goodbye and set off on the road to London. He carried nothing on his back, so as to travel the lighter, but plodded on with only a stick in his hand and the clothes he stood up in.

It took him four days to get to London, but as luck would have it, the weather cleared up, and he was able to spend the nights in barns or under haystacks. When he got to London, he had no difficulty in finding his way to the famous bridge, which in those days had houses and shops upon it, for there was always a great crowd of people going that way. As he got there, he took his stand at one end of the bridge and waited. He looked into the water and saw the boats passing, and he looked across the street and saw the coaches and waggons and people on horseback or on foot. But no one spoke to him. No one even noticed him. When night came, he made himself as comfortable as he could under the wall of a house and went to sleep.

Next day he tried the other end of the bridge, but it was just the same. Nobody took the slightest notice of him. When he felt hungry, he bought a small loaf of bread and some cheese and a mug of beer. So it went on, day after day, till at last he came to the end of his small supply of money.

'So this is the end of my adventure,' he said to himself, 'all the money gone and nothing to show for it. Not a soul has spoken to me. Not a word of news have I heard, common or marvellous. Now I must go home, and on the way I shall have to beg my bread, for I've scarcely twopence left.'

Just as he was about to take his last look at the great river and turn towards home, a shopkeeper from across the street strolled over and spoke to him.

'I can't help wondering who you are and what you want,' said he. 'I've noticed you standing on this bridge day after day. You've nothing to sell, you're no beggar, and you haven't spoken to a living soul; man, woman, or child. Tell me, if you will—just to satisfy my curiosity—what you are doing here?'

John hesitated. He did not like to tell a stranger why he had stood on London Bridge all that time doing nothing, but he was a simple fellow, and not good at thinking of lies and excuses, so at last he said:

'Well, to tell you the truth, neighbour, I am a poor country man, and three times I dreamed that if I came and stood on this bridge, I should hear wonderful news. But no such news have I heard, and now I have no money, so I must go home.'

The shopkeeper looked at him in astonishment, and then he began laughing. He laughed till the tears ran down his face and the pedlar thought he would burst his coat buttons.

'Why, what a fool you must be!' said the shopkeeper, as soon as he could find his voice. 'Do you mean to say you have come up to London from the country and stood all this time on the bridge, just because of an idle dream? You must be the simplest fellow that ever set foot in the city of London. What a story to tell my neighbours! What a tale to amuse my wife and keep her mind from the rheumatism that troubles her so sorely o'nights.'

Once more he roared with laughter.

'I tell you what, country fellow,' went on the shopkeeper, for he was a ready talker, 'why, the other night *I* had a dream too. Very clear and plain it was, but do you think I'm such an ass as to take heed of dreams? I dreamed of a voice, just like yourself; and this voice told me that if I was to go to some place called Swaffham in Norfolk—I think that was the place it said, but I can't exactly call it to mind, for I never heard of the place before—if I was to go to Swaffham, it said, and dig under an oak tree that grew behind a pedlar's cottage thereabouts, I should find a mighty great treasure. That's what I dreamed, fellow; but do you think I should be such a fool as to go all that way on account of a dream? Why, I don't even know it there's such a place as Swaffham in Heaven or earth!'

He had scarcely finished having his laugh at John's expense before the pedlar bid him good day very shortly and turned away to go home. The shopkeeper was surprised to find him depart at such speed. He took him to be an odd fellow, a little soft in the head, and thought no more of him.

As for John, he went off home as fast as he could, the words of the shopkeeper ringing in his ears. And the one thought that filled his mind during all the miles he had to trudge was of the oak tree at the bottom of his own garden which he knew so well. He should know it, too, for it was the very oak tree he had climbed every day as a boy, and which his own son had climbed in his turn.

At last, tired and hungry, he reached home. Glad indeed was his wife to see him safe and sound. No sooner had she given him a welcome than she went in to prepare him a meal. But hungry as he was, he did not stop to eat.

'Wife,' he said, 'bring me the spade we use to dig the garden with!'

'Why, here it is, John,' she said. 'It's a mercy I haven't sold it to buy bread with! What should you want with a spade? A very small spoon is all you'll need to eat what I've got for you, I'm thinking.'

But John did not hear her. He was digging furiously at the bottom of the garden, under the oak tree.

'Poor fellow,' said his wife to their two daughters, who had just come in to greet the pedlar, 'poor fellow! I'm afraid he had nothing else for the smart folks in London to steal, so they've stolen his wits—and much good may they get by it!'

But she was wrong. For after a few minutes' digging John laid bare a great wooden box, partly eaten away with mould, and all black with the earth and damp. He carried it indoors and opened it. When everyone saw what was in it, they could not speak for amazement. Inside the box was a great hoard of silver plate and gold coins, beside a few jewels and some precious ornaments of solid gold.

'I was right,' said John quietly. 'It was no lying voice, but the voice of truth itself. Now, what shall we do with all this?'

So, to show his thanks to God, he gave a great sum of money to repair the village church, which had fallen into decay; and with what was left, he and his family bought a fine big house and lived comfortably for the rest of their days.

CATSKIN

◆

There was once a proud gentleman, and he had a great house standing in the middle of a park. The park had fine trees, and there were deer roaming among them. He owned several farms and much land. But he had no children. Now, being such a proud gentleman, he wished above all to have a son who would bear his name when he was dead, and inherit all his land. Time passed, and at length his wife bore him a child. But you can imagine the gentleman's disappointment when he learnt that the child was a girl. A fine, healthy girl she was, but the gentleman was bitter and angry. So angry was he at not having a son, that he refused even to look at the baby girl.

'Never let her come in my sight!' he said. 'Take her away, and be careful that I never set eyes on her.'

So stern and fierce was the gentleman that his wife and the servants were obliged to obey him. As the little girl grew up, it was useless for them to tell him how beautiful, gay, and delightful she was. He could not even bear to hear her mentioned; and he could not forgive his wife for not having a son. It was not her fault, poor lady, but proud men are sometimes like that, and there was nothing she could do.

When the girl was fifteen years old, she was considered in those days old enough to be married. The gentleman gave orders that she was to marry the first man that came and asked for her. Now it happened that the first suitor was an old man with squint eyes and a cough. He had, besides, a thin, scraggy beard and bony knees that knocked together. The girl could not bear the thought of being married to him. So she went and talked to her friend the hen-wife. This was an old dame who lived in a cottage on the gentleman's land and brought eggs and poultry to the great house when they were wanted. She was thought by the people round about to be a witch, but the girl did not care about that. She always found her kind and helpful in times of trouble.

'What shall I do?' asked the girl. 'I don't mean to be married to that old scarecrow, but I don't know how to get out of it.'

'This is what you must do,' said the hen-wife. 'Tell them you will marry the old man, but that you must first have a dress of silver cloth.'

So the girl went back home and told them she must have a dress of silver cloth, and after a few days it was made. Very lovely she looked in it, but she still did not want to marry the old man.

'What shall I do?' she asked the hen-wife.

'Go back,' said the hen-wife, 'and tell them you must have a dress of beaten gold.'

So the girl went home and told them she must have a dress of beaten gold; and after a few days it was made for her, and everyone said they had never seen a girl more richly dressed. But still she did not want to marry the old man. So she went and talked to the hen-wife, and this time the hen-wife told her to ask for a dress made of feathers—one feather from each of the birds of the air. She went home and told them this; and a man went out with peas and scattered them on the ground.

'A feather for a pea!' he shouted to the birds of the air; and all the birds, from the tiny wren to the great eagle, from the drab sparrow to the gorgeous peacock, came and laid one of their feathers on the ground in exchange for a pea. When all the peas were gone, there was a great heap of feathers. And the dressmakers at the great house took the feathers and made them into a wonderful dress, and when the girl put it on, everyone said that never had they seen a bride more beautifully clothed.

But still she had no mind to marry the old man.

'What shall I do?' she asked her friend the hen-wife. 'I can't refuse much longer, and I am afraid they will make me marry him this time.'

'Everything will be all right,' said the hen-wife. 'This time you must ask for a dress made of catskin.'

So a dress was made from the skin of six black cats and seven tabby cats; and everybody was getting so impatient, especially the old man with the bony knees and the squint, that orders were given for the wedding to be held the very next day.

The girl did not stop to talk to the hen-wife any more; she decided to run away. It was the only thing to do. So that night she put on her dress of catskin, wrapped up her three other dresses in a bundle, and set out to walk away from her father's house as fast as the darkness would let her. Fortunately the moon was rising, so that she could see well enough to make her way through the woods. When she had been travelling for some time and had begun to grow weary, and the moon had set, leaving the woods very dark and eerie, she saw the lights of a great castle standing just at the edge of the wood. She stumbled upon a little hut belonging to a woodcutter, and here she left her bundle containing her three dresses. She hid them under pile of straw and old sacking; she hoped they would be safe there, for it did not look as if the hut were much used. Then she ate the little food she had brought with her, and lay down on the floor and went to sleep.

As soon as it was light, she went to the castle and found the kitchen entrance. She knocked at the door and asked to see the housekeeper. She told her she was looking for work, and the housekeeper said she could work as a scullery-maid as long as she was good, and she must take her orders from the cook. She would have all her meals and a bed to sleep on at night. So she took her place as scullery-maid in the great castle, and they all called her Catskin because of the dress she was wearing. Everyone liked her except the cook, who was a cruel, hard woman, jealous of Catskin because she was beautiful and everyone loved her.

One day the kitchen was in a great bustle with preparations for a ball that was to be held in the great hall to welcome back the young Lord who had just returned from the court in London. Never had there been such a stir! All the fine ladies and gentlemen of the countryside had been invited, and there were dishes to be prepared, silver and gold vessels to be cleaned and scoured, floors to be polished, and everything made trim and shining for the evening.

'How much I should like to go the ball,' said Catskin, and the cruel cook replied:

'What! A scullery-maid go to the ball! A fine figure *you* would make in your greasy old catskin among all the fine folks! Get on with your work, you impudent slut!'

With this she threw a basin of dirty water in Catskin's face, but Catskin only laughed and shook the water out of her eyes.

When evening came and her work was done, Catskin slipped out and went to the woodcutter's hut where she had left her fine dresses. She took off her dress of catskin and bathed herself in a crystal waterfall that sparkled nearby; then she combed her long golden hair and tied it back with a silver ribbon. She took her silver dress from the bundle and shook out the folds. So well had it been made, and so fine was the material, that it was scarcely creased at all. She put it on, fastened it at the neck, and ran back to the castle.

The guests had all arrived, and the gateway was crowded with coaches. Catskin could hear the music from the ballroom. Unnoticed, and a little bit afraid, she hurried up the great stairway and stepped proudly into the hall. For a few moments no one noticed her. The music drew to a close, and the dancers separated. Gradually a hush fell upon the crowded hall. The hush turned to a whisper. Everyone saw catskin in her silver dress, her eyes bright and her hair falling round her shoulders. Everyone wondered who she could be. Some of the young ladies bit their lips from jealousy; and the old ladies, who were sitting round the walls fanning themselves, remembered the days of their youth. They wondered if they could have been as beautiful as this unknown girl at their first ball. The young men stared at her; this was not good manners, but they could not help it. Then, the young Lord himself walked straight across the empty dancing-floor, bowed before her, and took her hand. In a few moments, the fiddlers struck up again, and the young Lord and Catskin led the dance.

All night Lord Marivel—for that was his name—danced with Catskin. He said little, but he could not take his eyes off her. As the very first grey of dawn began to show and some of the guests had already gone to find their coaches, Catskin told Marivel that she must go. He was in a dream and could hardly bring himself to bid her farewell.

'Where do you live?' he managed to ask her.

'Why,' said Catskin, 'at the sign of the Basin of Water.'

With that, she let go his hand and slipped through the crowd. Away she went to the hut under the trees and changed her silver dress for her dress of catskin. Next day, she was back at work in the castle kitchen, helping to wash the dishes and goblets after the great ball, just as if nothing had happened.

Lord Marivel asked everywhere for the sign of the Basin of Water, but no one had heard of it. He told his mother that he must find the girl with the silver dress, for he could not be happy without her, and he would never consent to marry anyone else. So inquiries were made, but nowhere could a trace be found of the young Lord's fair partner. After a while, his mother decided to hold another ball, in the hope that the unknown young lady would once more appear.

Again, everything was bustle in the kitchens. A second ball was to be held. Splendid dishes were prepared, and everything trimmed and polished as before.

'If only I might go to the ball,' sighed Catskin, and the cruel cook instantly replied:

'What! A scullery-maid go to a ball! A fine figure *you'd*

72

make among all the fine folks! Get on with your work, you impudent slut!'

So saying, she picked up a china ladle and broke it across Catskin's back. But the girl only laughed and ran off to fetch some more dishes.

However, Catskin was determined to go to the ball. When evening came, she hurried away to the hut under the trees and bathed herself in the crystal waterfall. Once more, she combed out her long golden hair until it gleamed like a sheaf of sunbeams. Then she changed her dress of catskin for her dress of beaten gold; and as soon as she was ready, she joined the throng of dancers in the great ballroom.

She had looked dazzling before in her silver dress but in her dress of beaten gold, she was more radiant than ever. A cry of wonder and amazement greeted her entrance. Lord Marivel instantly stepped up to her and claimed her as his partner. Once more they danced through the whole evening, and everyone said how handsome the young Lord was and how beautiful his partner. At last the ball wore to its end, and for the second time Catskin bid her partner goodnight and turned to go.

'But tell me,' Marivel pleaded, 'tell me where you live.'

'At the Sign of the Broken Ladle,' said Catskin with a laugh, and ran off leaving her partner in bewilderment, gazing after her.

Quickly she found the little hut, changed back into her catskin dress, and went back to her straw bed in the kitchen quarters.

As for Marivel, the same thing happened again. No one could tell him where to find the Sign of the Broken Ladle, and he began to pine for the sight of his sweet partner's face, her smiles and golden hair. So there was nothing for it but for his mother to order preparations for yet another ball, in the hope that Catskin would come as she had come to the other two.

A fortnight later, then, everyone in the great kitchen was bustling about, making ready for the ball.

'Oh, how I should like to go,' sighed Catskin.

'Oh, you would, would you?' sneered the cook. 'And a fine sight you'd be among all the fine folks in your dirty old catskin. Take that, you impudent hussy, and get on with your work!'

With that, she threw a metal carving fork at Catskin, but it missed her and hit the stone wall behind, falling to the floor with a clatter. Catskin only laughed and went on with her polishing.

That night, as you may guess, she stole out and bathed herself in the crystal waterfall, combed her long hair, and changed her catskin for the dress of birds' feathers.

What a sight she looked among the dancers in the ballroom! Even the musicians stopped to look at such an un-usual dress, and all the guests remarked that it suited her even better than the others had done.

Marivel danced with her the livelong night, and when she turned to go, once more he asked her to tell him where she lived.

'I live,' said she, 'at the Sign of the Crooked Carving Fork.'

But this time the young Lord was wiser. Following her to the door, he slipped on a dark cloak and went after her, unseen. Standing behind a tree in the faint light of morning, he saw her enter the woodcutter's hut and come out a few minutes later dressed in her catskin. Then he followed her back to the castle and saw her disappear through the kitchen entrance.

'So,' he said, 'this is where she lives all the time—under my very own roof!' and he could not help admiring her for the way in which she had avoided telling him she was employed in his mother's kitchen. But that did not trouble him in the least. He loved her whether she was a scullery-maid or a princess. It made no difference.

Next morning, he looked into the kitchen to make sure that Catskin was there, and no mistake. Sure enough, there she was, carrying dishes to the sink and singing to herself as she did so. It was all he could do not to take the dishes for her and carry them himself. But it would not do to frighten her away. So upstairs he went to see his mother and to tell her that he would never love any but the scullery-maid Catskin, who worked downstairs in her own castle.

'She is beautiful,' he said, 'and kind and gay, and no other will make me happy. If she will have me, I will marry her, no matter what people say.'

The lady of the castle talked it over with her lord, and he was very angry. He absolutely forbade his son to have anything to do with the scullery-maid, and told him that if ever he set eyes on her again, she would be sent away and told never to come near the castle again, on pain of death.

Very sadly, Marivel went up to his own room and lay on his bed. He knew it was useless to argue with his father. Yet he could scarcely believe that he was never to see Catskin again. He cared neither for food nor drink, but lay still on his bed, full of tormenting thoughts. He could not sleep at night, and before long he was pale and ill, and in a few days the castle doctor was seriously alarmed for his health.

The doctor told his master that the young Lord seemed

much troubled about a certain scullery-maid who worked in the kitchen, and that he refused to eat unless the food were brought to him by this very girl. Marivel's father was unwilling to let Catskin come near his sick son, but the doctor insisted that if he continued to eat nothing his health would be soon in great danger. So Catskin was allowed to bring Marivel his food. She did not speak to him, but simply gave him the dishes ordered by the doctor, giving him a curtsy and a grave smile as she did so. Gradually his strength returned, and the doctor told his father and mother that it was certainly Catskin who had brought about his recovery. It would be dangerous, he said, to separate Marivel and the young girl entirely.

When Marivel was quite recovered, he told his mother that he meant to marry Catskin, whatever his father said. His mother and father both reasoned and argued with him, but all in vain. In the end, the lady sent for Catskin. She changed into her dress of beaten gold and appeared before her mistress, curtsying modestly, but looking in no way ashamed. The lady was charmed with Catskin; there was something proud as well as humble, something shy as well as confident, in her bearing that made the lady feel that, after all, this girl would be no bad match for her son. Besides, everyone agreed that the girl was uncommonly beautiful in appearance, and graceful in all her movements. Her only fault was that she worked in the kitchen and was evidently not the daughter of a nobleman.

Well, to make a long story short, the lord and lady agreed to the match, and Marivel and Catskin were married with great splendour and ceremony. They lived happily together, and everyone agreed that there was not a more charming and well-matched pair in all the land.

But that was not the end. Catskin bore her husband a little son, and when he was four years old, a beggar woman called at the kitchen door and asked for some food for her own little boy, who was about the same age. Catskin's boy happened to be playing in the kitchen and, seeing the beggar woman's child, ran to greet him and kissed him fondly, smiling at him with evident pleasure and affection. Now the cruel cook still reigned over the kitchen. Catskin might have had her sent away to repay her for her unkindness in the past, but she was a soft-hearted girl, and had forgiven the cook her cruelty. The cook noticed the two little boys and said with a sneer:

'Just see how the two beggars' brats take to one another.'

Catskin overheard her, and her feelings were terribly hurt. She knew she was no beggar, but the daughter of a proud gentleman, quite as good as many of the Lord's own friends. Yet she wondered whether her husband was not secretly ashamed of her. He had never said anything, but Catskin felt that, after all, a husband has a right to know who his wife's parents are. So she told Marivel that she wished to go on a journey with himself and their young son. Next morning, they set off in a crimson coach drawn by four grey horses. After some hours upon the road, they arrived at the village near which was Catskin's old home. She had not been there since she had run away over five years ago. The coach put up at an inn in the village, and she and the little boy waited there while Marivel went to see if his wife's father was at home.

Marivel found the proud gentleman sitting by the fire in his great hall, miserable and alone.

'Kind sir,' he said, 'are you the father of a sweet girl who left home more than five years since, because she would have nothing to do with the man you had chosen for her husband?'

'I am that miserable man,' said the gentleman. 'I am a wicked and proud sinner, and I have paid a heavy price for my wickedness. I lost the sweetest child that ever a man had, and when she left home, my wife died from grief. So now I am all alone in the world, and I have nothing to hope for except death—and may God pardon me for my pride and cruelty. I wished for a son; and because I could not have one, I drove my daughter away.'

'Look at me,' said Marivel. 'Would you have thought me a fit son for such a gentleman as yourself?'

The gentleman raised his eyes and looked at the young Lord.

'Why, yes,' he said. 'You are a tall, handsome, and well-bred fellow; such a one as you would have been a son after my own heart. But what is the use of talking like this?'

'If I cannot be your son,' said Marivel, 'perhaps I might serve as the husband of your daughter. Sir, how would you like to see your daughter again, married to a man you approve, and with a little boy of her own to be your grandson?'

'Do not make fun of an old man,' said the gentleman. 'But if indeed you could bring such a miracle to pass, you would make me the happiest man in all the country.'

It did not take Marivel long to fetch his wife and son from the inn. How joyful Catskin was to see her father once more and to know that he bore her no malice! He clasped her in his arms and wept tears of joy, so that you might have found it hard to believe him the happiest man in all the country. Then he lifted his grandson in his arms, and the boy pulled his grey beard so hard that the gentleman wept even harder, while the boy crowed with delight.

After they had rested and dined, and Catskin had greeted her old friends among the servants, all four of them got into the crimson coach once more, and the four grey horses took them back to the castle. And there they lived happily ever afterwards, sometimes smiling over their adventures and sometimes crying a little over their misfortunes. As for the lord and lady, Marivel's parents, they were overjoyed to find that Catskin's father was a rich and respectable gentleman— for a gentleman is something, after all, even though he has been proud and foolish.

THE TULIP BED

❖

There was once an old woman who lived by herself in a cottage in the west country. She had a small garden in which grew roses and pinks, as well as salads and herbs for her table. But the pride of her garden was a tulip bed, which the old woman hoed and weeded with the utmost care, for she was very proud of her tulips. They were, indeed, a wonderful sight, and passers-by would never fail to stop and admire their delicate beauty. There were pink tulips, and red ones, yellow, white, and purple. They were tall, straight, and large-flowered, springing from their curled and pointed leaves, and swaying gently in the early summer air.

Now in those days there were little folk—or fairies, as the people called them—living in that part of the country, and one of their favourite haunts was a field just beyond the old woman's garden. They liked this field because it was never visited by meddling strangers. Here they could play undisturbed, dancing and singing under the trees in the moonlight. But one thing they found troublesome. On warm nights, when the moon was bright, they could not get their children to sleep. The small fairies would fidget and cry in their cots till their mothers grew almost frantic, fearing they would never be able to go and dance, but would have to sit up all night and sing them to sleep.

Then one fairy mother hit upon a new and clever plan. One evening, she carried her small baby across the field and into the cottage garden. Although the old woman was out in the garden bringing in the last of her clothes from the line, she did not see the fairy and her baby, for, of course, they were invisible to human eyes. The fairy flew with the baby over the tulip bed, and gently put it inside a yellow tulip. She hovered overhead, sang a little sleepy song, and as the tulip rocked in the evening breeze, the baby very soon fell fast asleep. The fairy mother flew home, changed quickly into her ball dress of thistledown and gossamer, and was the first to appear at the ball. Some unfortunate ones were not able to come till it was nearly over, because the night was very warm and their children more than usually tiresome.

Next night, all the mothers of babies took their children to the tulip bed and did as the first fairy had done. They chose tulips of their favourite colour and laid their children inside them. Soon soft lullabies sounded from all over the bed, and before long not a whisper was heard from the dozens of fairy babies asleep in the swaying flowers.

From this time on, the tulips grew even larger and straighter; their colours were richer and more delicate; what is more, the fairies even gave them a sweet scent, which is a thing no ordinary tulip has. The villagers noticed this, and some who had particularly keen ears even imagined they could hear the fairies singing when they passed that way at bedtime.

The old woman was astonished and delighted by the beauty of the flowers, and would never pick a single one. She let them grow and fade and live the natural course of their lives until they withered and the petals fell to the ground. She thought that the special loveliness of her tulips that year was due to the fineness of the season. But it was the same the next year, and the year after that; until at last she believed that the tulip bed was under the protection of the fairies—as indeed it was; for they continued to use the flowers as cradles for their babies and to dance and sing in the nearby field in honour of their queen.

Then at last, one cold winter, the old woman died. Her few things were sold, and the cottage was taken by a cross-grained man, who had no use for flowers and thought they took up ground that could be better used. So in the spring, what was the fairies' rage to find that he had uprooted and thrown away all the tulip bulbs and planted parsley in their place! Now they had nowhere to put their babies on fine moonlight nights, and the babies once more grew fretful and would not sleep. They had come to believe that the tulip bed was theirs by right. Fairies can be very angry and spiteful when human beings interfere with their rights, so they called a council and vowed vengeance on the cross-grained man. As soon as the warm sunshine made his parsley seeds sprout and show green tops, they caused them all to wither and die. Soon not a parsley sprout was left. So the cottager sowed the bed with onions, but the same thing happened again. Not an onion grew. Whatever he tried—carrots, cabbages, lettuces, spinach—it was always the same; nothing would flourish. At last, in despair, the cross-grained man left the bed to look after itself, and before long it was a mass of rank grass and tangled weeds. The fairies had lost for ever their tulip bed, and they had to think of other devices for getting their children to sleep.

But the fairies never forget those who have been kind to them. When the old woman had died, she had very few to mourn for her, and no one to plant flowers on her grave and keep it free from nettles and dandelions. She was so old when she died that soon afterwards all her old friends were dead too. So the fairies took it upon themselves to sing a funeral song for her in the churchyard each full moon, and to look after her grave. There she lay, peaceful and still in a corner of the churchyard, and at all seasons of the year fresh and sweet flowers grew on the grave, and never a weed showed its head. Thus they continued for many years, and people marvelled that in all the churchyard that one grave should always be fresh and well cared-for, though no human hand was ever seen to plant flowers or pull up weeds. And as it happened, the one to sing the sweetest at full moon over the old woman's grave was the very fairy who, when a baby, had been the first to be rocked asleep in the yellow tulip.

SIMPLETON PETER

❖

There was once a young man called Peter, who lived in a country village with his old widowed mother. He was a good-hearted fellow, tall and strong, but he was one of the simplest of men ever born. He could scarcely count his mother's hens, though she had only a score; if he spent threepence out of a shilling, he hardly knew how to work out the change; and as for going to market, he never went without being cheated. It was not for want of trying; it was not because he was lazy; it was just that poor Peter seemed to have been born with scarcely any brains in his head.

'Oh, Mother,' he would say, 'if only I'd been given just a wee bit of brains, I'd not be so much trouble and worry to you.'

'Ay, Peter,' his mother would say, with a sigh, 'you're short of brains, there's no doubt, but you're a good boy, and as strong as any other two, so don't you let it worry you. Now run upstairs and get me three buttons to sew on your jacket, and mind you, three is three and not two, nor four neither.'

All the same, Peter used to fret about his foolishness. So he continued to pester his mother till at last she said:

'Well, if you want to come by some brains, just take a walk

to the wise woman who lives on the hill. She's a right clever body, they say, with her magic books and her pills and potions, and perhaps she can help you.'

So when his work was done, Peter walked up the hill, and on the top he found the cottage of the wise woman, with smoke coming out of the chimney and a black cat stretched out asleep in the doorway.

'Well, that's a good sign,' said Peter to himself, and knocked at the door.

There was no answer, so he lifted the latch cautiously and looked in. There was the old woman, stirring a round black pot on the fire. She neither turned nor said a word, so Peter stepped inside and said:

'Good day to you, wise woman. 'Tis a very fine day, to be sure.'

The old woman said nothing, but went on stirring.

'Maybe we shall have rain tomorrow,' Peter went on.

But still the old woman said nothing.

'And maybe we shan't,' he added, wondering what to say next.

Still the old woman went on stirring.

'Well now,' said Peter, 'that's all I have to say about the weather, so let's come to business. I'm a very simple fellow, and I came to see whether you could supply me with a wee bit of brains. You see—'

'Brains?' said the old woman, putting down her spoon and turning round for the first time. 'Yes, I dare say. That depends on what sort of brains you want. If it's king's brains, or soldier's brains, or schoolmaster's brains, then I can't help you. What sort of brains do you want?'

'Just ordinary brains,' said Peter. 'Middling good, and mid-dling bad, like most of the folks round here.'

'Very good,' said the wise woman. 'Such brains you shall have, but you must fetch me the heart of the thing you like above all others. Do you understand? And when you have brought me that, you must answer me a riddle, so that I may tell whether you have really brought the thing I ask for. Now be off with you.'

Without waiting for an answer, she took up the pot and car-ried it into the back kitchen, leaving Peter to let himself out. He went off down the hill, thinking about what the wise woman had said. 'The heart of thing I like above all others,' he repeated to himself. 'Now what can that be, I wonder?' For this was not the sort of thing Peter usually thought about. When he got home, he told his mother what the old woman had said, and his mother thought the question over. At last she said:

'Why, there's nothing in this world you like better than fat bacon, if you ask me. So we'd best kill the old sow, and you can take its heart to the wise woman.'

So the old sow was killed and her heart removed, and Peter took it next evening to the cottage on the hill.

The wise woman was sitting in a chair by the fireplace reading a great book. She scarcely looked up, and Peter put the heart down on the table.

'There 'tis,' he said. 'The heart of the thing I like best in all the world. Will it do?'

The old woman looked up from her book.

'What is it,' she said, 'that can run without feet? Tell me that.'

'What is it that can run without feet?' repeated the young

man, and he scratched his head, and thought and thought till his head ached.

The old woman went on reading. At last Peter spoke.

'I tell you what,' he said. 'I dunno.'

'Well, that's not the thing I asked for,' said the old woman. 'Take it away and be off with you.'

There was nothing for poor Peter to do but pick up the sow's heart and go home again.

When he got near his own cottage, he saw there were people standing about the doorway, and some of the women were crying. Then he learnt that his old widowed mother had been taken suddenly ill and was near death. He went inside the cottage and closed the door. The old woman was indeed very feeble. Peter saw there was nothing to be done, so he knelt by the bedside and took her hand.

'Say goodbye to me, son,' she whispered, 'for I'm going to leave you. But now you've been to the wise woman and got yourself some brains, you'll be able to look after yourself.'

Peter had not the heart to tell her that he had got no brains and had not even been able to answer the wise woman's riddle. Instead, he kissed his mother and said:

'All the same, Mother, I shall miss you badly. Goodbye, Mother dear, goodbye.'

'Goodbye, my son,' said the old woman; and with that she closed her eyes, smiled at him faintly, and died.

Peter stayed for a long while kneeling by the bed, crying and crying, for he could not stop the tears from coming. And he thought of all she had done for him—how she had brought him up as a little boy, and healed his cuts when he fell over, and cooked his meals, and mended his clothes, and talked to him, and been company for him in the evenings. He wondered how in the world he would get on without her. 'For,' he said to himself, 'of all creatures in the world, she was the one I liked best.'

Then he thought of the wise woman's words.

'Bring me,' she had said, 'the heart of the one you like best in all the world.'

'That I shan't,' he said, 'not for all the brains on earth.'

But next morning he thought he might take his dead mother up to the old woman without taking her heart out, for he was even more in need of a bit of brains than ever. So he put his mother in a sack and took her up the hill. This he did without difficulty, for his mother had been a frail little woman, and he himself was as strong as any two ordinary men. He laid the body down in the wise woman's cottage and said:

'Now this time I have surely brought you the thing I love above all others. Here is my very own dead mother, and now you must give me the brains you promised.'

'Tell me this,' said the wise woman. 'What is it that is yellow and shines and isn't gold?'

'What's it that is yellow and shines and isn't gold?' Peter said in a dazed way. 'Why—'

But he couldn't think of the answer for the life of him, so at last he said:

'I dunno.'

'Then you shall get no brains today. You're a simple fellow indeed, and maybe you'll never have any at all.'

So Peter took up the sack with his mother inside and went out. But he was too sad to go home; instead, he sat down by the roadside and began to cry.

Presently, he heard the sound of a gentle voice at his side. He looked up and saw a handsome young girl watching him with a kindly smile.

'What's the matter?' she asked. 'I'm sorry to see a great fellow like you in distress.'

'I'm a simple fellow,' said Peter, 'without any brains, and now my mother has died and left me all alone. So how I'll manage from now on I don't know. There's no one to cook for me and sew for me and manage the marketing, and worst of all, there's no one to talk to me and cheer me up when I'm in trouble.'

'I'll help you,' said Jenny, for this was the girl's name. 'A simple fellow like you shouldn't be without someone to look after him. Will you let me come and look after you?'

'If you like,' said Peter, 'but you'll find I'm a more than commonly stupid man, unless I can get some brains from somewhere.'

'Well,' said Jenny, 'they say that a foolish man makes the best husband. Will you marry me?'

'Can you cook?' said Peter.

'Yes, indeed,' said Jenny.

'Can you sew and mend clothes?'

'To be sure.'

'Can you count eggs and add up pounds, shillings, and pence?'

'Well enough.'

'Then, if you'll marry me, I'll have you,' agreed Peter.

Off they went, and after Peter's mother had been buried and all the village had mourned for her, the two of them were married and made their home together in the cottage. Soon

Peter, simple as he was, began to see that he had got a very good wife. She cooked and sewed, mended and washed, all with the greatest cheerfulness and good will. What is more, she kept Peter amused with her witty talk and her gentle ways. Peter was not a bad husband either, for he, too, worked cheerfully and well; nothing was too much trouble for him, so long as he did not have to think; no weight was too much for him to lift, and no distance was too great for him to walk. In short, they were as happy and contented a couple as had ever set up house together in the village.

'Why, Jenny,' said Peter one evening, 'I believe that of all creatures in the world, you're the one I like the best.'

And these words put an idea into his head.

'Surely,' he went on, 'the wise woman didn't mean me to kill you and take her your heart. Do you think she could have meant that, Jenny?'

'I hope not,' said his wife, 'indeed I do. Who said anything about killing? Why not take me up to her, alive as I am, heart and all?'

'That's a very good notion,' said Peter. 'Why couldn't I have thought of it myself? Just you come along with me. But first, you'd better see if you can answer riddles. Tell me, what is it that can run without legs?'

'Why, a river, to be sure,' said Jenny. 'That's not very hard.'

'A river?' repeated the simpleton. 'Of course. Now why couldn't I have thought of that? But tell me this: what is it that shines and is yellow, but isn't gold?'

'The sun,' said Jenny, without stopping to think. 'I could have told you that when I was five years old.'

'The sun?' said Peter in a puzzled way. 'Yes—that shines, to be sure; and 'tis yellow; and 'tisn't gold neither. Why, what a head you have, Jenny! There can't be a man in all England with a cleverer wife than I have. Come along quickly now, and see if the old woman will give me a little bit of brains, so that I can be more your equal.'

So they went up the hill together, and found the wise woman at home.

'Wise woman,' said Peter, 'at last I've brought you the creature I like above all others. Here she is, heart and all. If you don't give me the brains I ask for now, you're no wise woman, but a cheat and a fraud.'

'Sit down, both of you,' said the old woman. They sat down, and she turned to Peter and said, 'Now then, here's my riddle. See if you can answer it. What is it that has first no legs, then two, then four?'

Poor Peter thought and thought, but the answer would not come; then Jenny whispered in his ear:

'A tadpole. Say, a tadpole.'

'A tadpole,' said Peter promptly; and the old woman said:

'Right. Now I see you've got all the brains you want, and they are inside your wife's head. If a man has a clever wife, she is all the brains he needs. Now be off with you, and don't come bothering me any more.'

Peter and Jenny got up, thanked the old woman, and went on their way.

As they went down the hill, Jenny was singing quietly to herself, but Peter said nothing.

'What are you thinking of?' she asked gently, stopping in the middle of a song.

Peter left off scratching his head and said nothing. At last he turned to her and answered:

'I was only thinking how proud I am to have such a more than commonly clever young wife. To be sure, you told the old woman just what she wanted to know. All the same,' he went on in his puzzled way, 'all the same, I *can't* see just why it should be a tadpole that has first no legs, then two legs, then four. I've puzzled it out and I've puzzled it out, and still I can't understand. I just can't understand.'

THE WELL OF THE THREE HEADS

———————— ❖ ————————

The King of Colchester had a daughter called Joanna, who was fifteen years old, and very sweet and gentle. They loved one another dearly, for the King had no wife; she had died ten years ago. Being in want of money, the King at last married a rich lady, who was ugly, ill-tempered, and spiteful. And the rich lady had a daughter of Joanna's own age. She was called Isabel; but instead of being like her step-sister, she was plain, spiteful, and surly, just like her mother. It was an evil day when the King brought such a graceless pair to Colchester, all for the sake of their riches.

Well, no sooner were the new Queen and her spiteful daughter settled down than they began to turn the King's mind against his own daughter. They said unkind things about her behind her back, and the King, who was anxious to please his new wife because she had brought him so much money, believed them. At last Joanna was so unhappy that she asked her father if she might go out into the world and seek her fortune.

'Father,' she said, 'I do not seem to be able to please my stepmother and Isabel; you do not need me any more. You would all be happier if I went. I shall miss you, but when I have made my fortune, I will come back and see you.'

'Very well,' said the King, 'if you want to go, go you shall. I will not stand in your way, for I can see that you are not happy here.'

And the King sighed deeply as if he, too, were unhappy and had perhaps begun to feel sorry that he had married again and brought such trouble into his palace. But what could he do?

'You will be well able to look after yourself,' he said to Joanna. 'Go to your stepmother and ask her to give you provisions for the journey.'

The Queen gave her nothing but a coarse bag of sacking containing dry bread and a small bottle of ale. She was glad that Joanna was going away. She gave her a kiss on the cheek that was more like a peck and told her to be good and look after herself. But truly she did not care what became of her. Joanna bade her father goodbye and set off to make her fortune.

Through the fields and woods she went, sad at heart; yet soon she began to sing, for the sun was shining and there was a warm breeze blowing through the leaves. Presently she came upon an old man sitting by the roadside.

'Where are you off to?' said he. 'And what have you got in that bag?'

'Only bread and ale,' she said, 'but you can have some if you like.'

'Thank you, my dear,' said the old man, 'I would dearly like to share your food, for I have had nothing to eat this day.'

So Joanna sat down beside him on the green bank and shared her crusts and her bottle with him. When they had finished, the old man said to her:

'You will presently come to a thick thorn-hedge, and you will not be able to get through.'

'Then what shall I do?' asked Joanna.

'Take this wand,' said the old man, giving her a hazel-twig which he had in his hand, 'and when you come to the hedge, wave it, and the hedge will open and let you through.'

'Thank you,' said Joanna, taking the wand, 'that is very kind of you.'

'No kinder than you have been to me,' said the old man. 'I wish you good day and good fortune.'

So Joanna went on her way, and presently she came to a thorn-hedge, just as the old man had said. Never had she seen such a fierce, prickly hedge in her life. But she did as she had been told, waved the wand three or four times in front of the hedge, and waited. In a few moments it opened wide enough to let her pass. She stepped through the gap, and the hedge closed behind her.

In a little while she came to a well, and from it arose the sound of voices wailing and singing. Joanna bent to look down, and as she did so, a head rose from the water and spoke to her. It was the head of a fair young woman with shut eyes and long, tangled hair; the mouth opened and spoke to Joanna. This is what it said:

> *'Wash me and comb me, and lay me down gently,*
> *That I may be comely for passers to see.'*

So Joanna sat down beside the well and took the head gently in her lap, and she thought that a look of gratitude came over the face. With the cloth that covered her own head she wiped the face softly; then with her comb she smoothed the wet, tangled hair. After that, she placed the head upon a bank of primroses.

Then another head rose out of the well, tangled and sad; and it, too, sang the words:

> '*Wash me and comb me, and lay me down gently,*
> *That I may be comely for passers to see.*'

Joanna took it in her lap, wiped the face, smoothed the hair, and laid the head down among the primroses.

Next, a third head came out of the well and sang:

> '*Wash me and comb me, and lay me down gently,*
> *That I may be comely for passers to see.*'

Joanna did as she had done with the other two heads, and when all three were lying side by side on the bank, the first head spoke.

'What shall we give this Princess to reward her for her kindness? I shall give her the gift of beauty, so that all men shall look at her and a great king take her for his wife.'

'And I shall give her the gift of a sweet voice,' said the second head, 'so that all will long to hear her speak and sing.'

'And I shall give her riches,' said the third head, 'so that she will have something to give to the man that weds her.'

Then they told Joanna to put them back in the well, and this she did, tenderly and carefully, so as not to hurt them; and as they sank into the water, she heard them sighing sleepily.

Then Joanna went on her way singing, and it seemed as if her voice was lovelier than that of a bird; for as she passed a holly-bush where a blackbird was singing, it stopped to listen to her. Perhaps, too, her face was more lovely than ever, for a young deer that was trotting through the wood stopped to look at her. He was panting heavily, as if he had been pursued; but on seeing Joanna he stopped, and two tears trickled down the side of his nose. She felt sorry for him and put her arms round his neck. At this moment, there was the sound of a hunting horn, and some men rode along the path. One had a bow and arrow raised to shoot, but on seeing the girl, he lowered it. Then the leader of the party rode up to Joanna. He had a splendid black horse with a richly embroidered saddle-cloth, and his own clothes were rich and fine.

He told her he was a king and that he was out hunting. Joanna begged him to spare the young deer because it looked so sad and was out of breath. The King looked at her, and her beauty touched his heart as nothing had touched it before. The sweetness of her voice, too, made him shy and gentle. All at once, he felt as if he were tired of hunting and had no wish to pursue the trembling deer.

'It shall go free,' he told her. 'You, too, look tired. If you will ride my horse, I will be glad to walk at your side.'

Joanna let go of the deer, and it bounded off between the trees; the King told his men not to follow it, but instead to ride back to his castle and bid them make ready for a guest.

Joanna knew well how to ride horseback. The King lifted her into the saddle, and with his hand on the bridle he led her along the pathway.

Presently he told her that he loved her for her sweet voice, and even more for her beauty, and even more for her gentleness and her kind heart.

'If you will have me,' he said, 'I will make you my Queen, and together we will reign over my kingdom.'

'The bride of such a king as you,' she said, 'must bring a rich dowry; and I have nothing—nothing at all. My father is poor, and my stepmother will give me nothing.'

'I will wed you without a dowry,' said the King. 'I have money enough, and I love you for yourself alone.'

'Nevertheless,' said Joanna, 'I wish I had something. For the bride who brings her husband nothing may not please his friends.'

'What have you there in your sack?' asked the King.

Joanna had not noticed that she still had the old sack that her stepmother had given her.

'Nothing but a few crusts, I fear,' she said, but she put her hand inside, and to her astonishment she brought out pearl necklaces, jewels, and rich ornaments.

'Why, this is a fortune,' said the King. 'I would have had you with nothing but the crusts, but your goodness has turned them into pearls. Now no one shall say that you came to me with nothing.'

Well, Joanna married the young King amid great rejoicing; they were very happy, for the King was kind and handsome, and Joanna was beautiful and sweet-voiced, and all the people loved her and were glad that their King had made such a wise choice. Soon they decided to pay a visit to Joanna's father, the King of Colchester; she had long been thinking about him and wondering how he was getting on without her. They got into a wonderful state coach drawn by four white horses which trotted gracefully along the high road towards Colchester.

Great was the ugly stepmother's surprise to see such a splendid coach arrive in the courtyard below her window. How angry she was, and how jealous when she found who was in it! And how delighted the poor King of Colchester was! He had missed his daughter sorely, and was deeply sorry that he had married such a spiteful and cross-grained Queen. The Queen was even angrier and more jealous when she saw how beautiful Joanna had become, how handsome and noble her husband was, and how rich and happy they both were. She determined to get such a husband for her daughter, ugly and spoilt though she was.

After they had all sat down together to a meal, Joanna told her father and stepmother the whole story of how she had met the old man by the roadside, seen the three heads at the well, and found her husband in the woods.

'Isabel shall go the very same way tomorrow,' the Queen said. 'I see no reason why she should not get as good a fortune as Joanna—better, perhaps. I am sure she deserves much better. What do you think?' she asked the King.

'I expect you are right,' said the King; and the very next day the Queen took a fine soft leather bag and put delicate cakes and pastry in it, and a flask of the finest white wine from Spain. She gave this to Isabel, wished her good fortune, and sent her on her way.

When Isabel came to the place where Joanna had seen the old man, sure enough there he was, just as before.

'Good day to you,' said the man pleasantly. 'Where are you going, and what have you in that fine leather bag?'

'What's that to you, old man?' said Isabel rudely.

'Why, nothing, to be sure, except that I have had nothing to eat since yesterday, and if you had a crust or a cake to spare an old man, I would be glad to wish you good fortune.'

'I have nothing for beggars,' said the surly Isabel, and went on her way.

Presently she came to the thick thorn-hedge, now fiercer and more formidable than ever. Isabel could see no way round, so, covering her face with her hands, she forced her way through. But the thorns, as if they hated such an ill-tempered and uncharitable girl, scratched her arms and tore at her hair and her ankles. Moreover, Isabel's mother had given her fine, costly clothes, and these were now torn and rent by the thorn-hedge. So, covered with blood and scratches, she struggled out on the other side, and began to look for water to wash herself in.

She came to the well of the three heads, and was about to dip her hands in when one of the heads appeared above it. Its hair was once more tangled and its face smeared.

> 'Wash me and comb me, and lay me down gently,
> That I may be comely for passers to see.'

'I'll do no such thing,' said Isabel, 'I am the one that needs washing and combing. Get back where you came from!'

And she gave it a knock with her bottle.

Then the other two heads appeared, one after the other, and asked the same favour; and Isabel treated them in the same manner. So the three heads got close together and asked one another how they could bring ill-fortune on such a cruel girl. Well, the first one covered her skin with leprosy, and the second gave her a harsh, grating voice like a rusty gate, and the third promised that her husband should be a poor cobbler with a squint whom nobody else would have. Poor Isabel! Evil though she was, you would have been sorry to see her hideous white skin and hear her grating voice. But the people in the market town were not sorry for her; as soon as she got there they were frightened and ran away in all directions, for they did not want her to give them her leprosy. The only man who did not turn and run when Isabel arrived was a poor cobbler with a squint eye who sat mending a shoe on the cobblestones.

'Oh, help me, help me!' cried Isabel. 'Where can I find one to cure me of this horrible disease? I have money and will pay him well.'

'If I cure you of your disease,' said the cobbler, 'will you marry me? That is the price I ask.'

'Yes, yes, I will marry you,' said Isabel. 'Only help me quickly!'

Now the cobbler had once mended some shoes for a poor hermit, and the hermit had given him a pot of ointment for the leprosy and a bottle of oil that would cure a grating voice. He gave Isabel the ointment, and with this her skin was cured; and he gave her the oil, and with this her harsh voice was cured. Then he took her home and married her.

In a few days' time they set off to visit Isabel's mother and stepfather. In the King's palace at Colchester everyone was enjoying a splendid banquet—a farewell banquet to Joanna and her husband, who were going to their own home the following day. How surprised the Queen was when she saw, not a fine carriage with delicate white horses and jewelled reins, but a villainous-looking cobbler with a squint, and on his arm her own daughter Isabel! At first the Queen could hardly speak for anger and spite.

'Where did you get that dreadful-looking man?' she screamed at last. 'And why are you not beautiful, like my stepdaughter? Why is your voice not sweeter than a nightingale, and why have you not married a great king with a coach and eight horses?'

Then the Queen choked and was ill and had to be carried to her room. But she never recovered from the shock, and soon afterwards died of anger and grief.

The King of Colchester thought that the cobbler was a very good husband for his stepdaughter Isabel, but he could not forgive Isabel for having made Joanna unhappy; so he told the cobbler that he would give him a hundred pounds to set himself up in a shop, if he would take his wife to live in a distant part of the country, as far from Colchester as possible. So off they went with their hundred pounds, and they were as good as their word and did not trouble the King any more.

After that the King went for a time to stay with his daughter Joanna and the young King, and many happy times they had together; so that after a while they were all able to forget the trouble which had been caused by the rich and spiteful stepmother.

JACK AND THE BEANSTALK

——— ❖ ———

Once upon a time there was a poor widow who lived in a cottage with her only son, Jack. Jack was a clever boy—strong, good-natured, and ready with his hands; but he did not go out and work for a living, staying at home instead and helping his mother about the house and garden. He chopped wood to make the fire, dug and weeded the little vegetable patch, and milked their one cow, Milky White. The widow cooked and cleaned and mended, so that the two of them, though they were poor, lived in contentment and had enough to eat and drink.

Now one year, after a hard, cold spring, there was a dry summer, and the grass in the meadow withered; so that Milky White gave no milk. Jack and his mother were soon without butter, nor had they milk to drink and to sell. Their vegetables did not grow because of the dry weather, and they were forced to spend the little money they had saved.

'Jack,' said his mother, 'I think we had better sell Milky White. She will soon die if she can get no grass, and we must have money for food and drink.'

·'Very well, Mother,' said Jack. 'I will take her to market, and with the money I get, we will buy goods to start a shop. We can get dishes and mugs, and laces and thread, and penny books and things of that sort that our neighbours need; and soon we shall be rich. You shall see. Tomorrow is market-day, and I shall set off first thing in the morning.'

'I shall be sorry to lose Milky White,' sighed the widow, 'but go she must. Get a good price for her, mind you—not less than ten pounds, or twelve perhaps.'

'Not a penny less than fifteen,' said Jack, 'and don't be surprised if I come back with twenty.'

So next morning, when he had what little breakfast his mother could provide, Jack drove Milky White out of the field and down the lane which used to be full of puddles and mud but was now baked dry and hard as a biscuit. He broke himself a switch from the hedge and gave the cow a touch on her side every now and then to keep her moving. Presently they reached the high road, and off they went towards the market town.

They had not been going long when they met a queer old man bent nearly double and tapping his way along with a stick. He looked up as Jack drew near, and Jack saw that he had very bright and twinkling eyes.

'Good day,' he said, for he was always a friendly boy.

'Good day, young man,' said the traveller, 'and where are you off to this bright day?'

'I am off to market to sell my cow,' Jack told him.

'Oh, indeed,' said the old man. 'I wonder what sort of a bargain you'll make. Let's see if you're as smart as you look. Can you tell me how many beans make five?'

'Why, that's not hard,' laughed Jack, thinking the old man

was a bit simple. 'Two in my left hand, two in my right hand, and one in my mouth.'

'Right you are. Now just come here, young man.'

So Jack went closer to the bright-eyed fellow, who put his hand in his wallet and drew out five beans.

'And there they are,' he said. 'How would you like them in exchange for the cow?'

'What! Five beans in exchange for Milky White?' asked Jack. 'What sort of a bargain do you call that?'

'Ah!' said the old man. 'These are no common beans. Just plant them, and they'll grow right up to the sky. You look the sort of young fellow that has a mind for marvels and mysteries and such like. Have you ever heard of such a marvel as that, now?'

Well, Jack said he hadn't; but how was he to know whether the beans were truly magical, as the old man had said?

'I'll tell you what,' said the man. 'Just you take the beans and give me the cow; and if the beans aren't as I say, meet me here tomorrow at the same time, and you shall have the cow back again, and no harm done.'

Jack thought this was a fair offer, so without more argument, he took the beans and handed Milky White's halter over to the bright-eyed man. He had forgotten all about the fifteen or twenty golden pounds he was to take home to his mother, and thought of nothing but the wonderful beans that were going to grow up to the sky. So off went the old man with Milky White, and back home went Jack with the five beans safely in the pocket of his trousers.

Jack's mother was surprised to see him home so early.

'Well,' she said, 'bless me! I see you've sold Milky White—and a good price you must have got for her or you wouldn't be back so soon. How much? Ten? Fifteen? Don't say it was twenty! A good cow she was to be sure, but—'

'Mother,' interrupted Jack, 'I got no money for her at all. After all, Mother, anybody can get *money*—but just you wait till you see what I did get.'

'No money!' said the widow. 'No money? You let Milky White go for nothing, then, you foolish boy?'

'Not for nothing,' said Jack. 'Just you look here. This is what I got for her.'

So saying, he pulled the five beans out of his pocket and put them into his mother's hand.

'Is that all?' she said, hardly able to believe her eyes. 'Beans? You take my only cow to market, and all you bring home is a few dried-up, miserable, good-for-nothing—'

'They're not ordinary beans, Mother,' said Jack. 'They're magic beans!'

Jack's mother was a good-tempered woman, but this time she was really angry.

'Magic fiddlesticks!' she cried. 'Why, you poor foolish, ignorant vagabond—you've been cheated, that's what! Now we are ruined, and I shan't live to see the end of your disgrace. Why, these aren't even fit to make soup of! Get to bed, you blockhead, this instant. There's no supper for such a dolt, nor ever likely to be from this day on.'

So without giving Jack a chance to speak up for himself, she threw the beans out of the window and fairly pushed the boy upstairs to his little room and slammed the door after him.

Poor Jack lay down on his bed and began to think how

foolish he had been. He was sorry, too, to think how greatly he had disappointed his old mother, and what a useless good-for-nothing she must think him! Hungry as he was, he hardly missed his supper, and in a little while, without bothering to undress, he fell asleep.

2

In the morning, Jack was amazed to find the room filled with a pale-green light, and at first he thought he must be dreaming. Then he heard the well-known sound of the neighbour's cock crowing and the barking of the old sheep-dog from the farm-yard over the way. Looking towards the window, he saw that it was covered with a pattern of broad green leaves growing from strong, twisting stems. They looked like—yes, they *were*—bean leaves! The magic beans! What had happened to them?

He jumped up from the bed and ran to the window. Of course! His mother had tossed them into the garden the evening before, and they must have sprouted in the night. Then they were magic! He threw open the window and looked down. There, sprouting from the ground below, was a strong ladder of beanstalks, twisting and twining together, with strong green leaves growing out all round. Then he looked up. Yes, the beanstalk grew right up—up and up to the very sky. The top was lost in the clouds.

Without stopping to think, Jack climbed on to the window-sill and tested his weight on the beanstalk. It bore him easily. At once he started to climb up. He was a good climber, and not in the least afraid of heights. Up and up he went, climbing, climbing, climbing—climbing, climbing, climbing, till he could look down and see his mother's cottage far away below, with a wisp of blue smoke rising lazily from the chimney and some dish-cloths drying on the garden hedge. Soon he was lost in the clouds.

On top of the clouds, the sun shone brilliantly; stretching away out of sight there was a broad, white road. Jack stepped off the beanstalk-ladder and began to walk along the road. Not a man, not a beast, not a house was in sight. Now and again a strange bird flew past. Otherwise there was no sign of life.

Just when Jack was beginning to think the road would go on forever, he saw in the distance a tall, tall house; and when he got closer, a tall, tall woman came out of the door with a pail in her hand. Jack hurried up to the house and asked the woman, as bold as brass, if she could give him some breakfast.

'Run away from here, little boy!' she cried. 'For it's no breakfast you'll get, but it's breakfast you'll *be*! My man is an ogre—a great big tremendous ogre, as fierce as ten tigers, and it's mighty fond he is of a boy like yourself, grilled on toast with a piece of butter on top to make him tender!'

'Well, ma'am,' said Jack. 'I'm starving with hunger, and there's no food for me at home. If you can spare me a bite of breakfast, I don't care if I'm eaten myself afterwards.'

Well, the ogre's wife was not a bad sort, though she had been hardened by having an ogre for a husband. So she looked round to see if the ogre was in sight, then pushed Jack in at the door, sat him down in the kitchen, and gave him some bread and cheese and a mug of new milk.

Just as Jack was finishing his breakfast, there came a terrible noise, and the house began to shake. Thump, thump, thumpety thump! It was the ogre coming home.

'Quick!' said the woman. 'Into the oven with you! He won't look there. If he catches sight of you, he'll make no more than three mouthfuls of you, or maybe two.'

So into the great oven jumped Jack, and the ogre's wife slammed the door after him, just as the ogre came into the kitchen. He was carrying three dead calves on his belt, and he flung them down on the table and told his wife to cook them for his breakfast. Then he looked round and sniffed. Snuff, snuff, sniff! Jack could hear him through the oven door, though it was made of cast iron with solid brass knobs. And then he heard the ogre's great voice shouting:

> 'Fee, fi, foh, fum!
> I smell the blood of a British man.
> Be he alive, or be he dead,
> I'll grind his bones to make my bread!'

Ogres have very sharp noses, and he must have smelt the smell of Jack. But his wife said:

'Nonsense, now! It's nothing but the smell of the boy you had last night for supper. Sit you down and take your boots off, and I'll have your breakfast ready in two shakes.'

Well, the ogre took his boots off, and his wife cooked the three calves for his breakfast; and after breakfast the ogre went to an iron-bound chest that stood against the wall and took out three bags of gold. He emptied them on the table and began to count them. When he had counted the gold, he put it back into the bags; but he was sleepy with going out all night in search of his breakfast, and presently he started to doze. After a bit, he began snoring, and Jack heard his snores through the door of the oven, even though it was of cast iron with knobs of solid brass. The ogre's snores were like ten thunderstorms in the mountains during the hot, hot days of August when the land is covered with drought and all the river-beds are dusty and parched. Then the ogre's wife opened the door of the oven and let Jack out.

'You'd best get along as quick as you can,' she whispered. 'It's asleep he is, and Heaven help you if he wakes before you're away.'

Jack's sharp eyes had caught sight of the three money-bags on the table, and while the woman's back was turned, he grabbed one of them and ran out of the door as fast as he could go. With the bag of gold clutched in his hand, he sped back along the broad white road till he came to the beanstalk. He looked back and saw that he was not being followed; then he stepped on to the beanstalk and climbed down as fast as he could. As he did so, he dropped the bag of gold, and of course it fell right into his mother's garden.

'Lord-a-mercy!' she cried as the bag burst asunder at her feet. ' 'Tis a long time I've lived, and a many things I've seen, but never before has it rained gold pieces on a fine summer morning. *And* boys!' she added, as Jack came flying down the beanstalk just as she was beginning to pick up the gold.

'Well, Mother,' said he, clasping her in his arms and dancing round with her all over the onion bed, 'what do you think of your idle, good-for-nothing, dunder-headed, ignorant, stupid son *now*? I hope these little bits of gold I've brought down from the sky will help to keep the wolf from the door.'

The old woman admitted that her son was smarter than she had thought, though, of course, she had known all along that he was smarter than most sons. The beans had turned out to be not such a bad bargain after all—though, of course, if *she* hadn't had the sense to drop them out of the window right on a patch of good soil, they might never have sprouted at all.

Well, off they went to the town and bought Jack's mother a new black dress, and a couple of fine hams to eat, and a pony and trap to go home in, and a set of new dishes, and a brand new axe and a pocket-knife, and a few more things such as a boy needs. And for a long time they lived in comfort and happiness on the gold pieces that Jack had brought home from the ogre's house. They never lacked meat and drink; and all their time was taken up with using the fine, new things they had wanted so long and were now able to buy.

3

Even a bag of gold does not last for ever, and the time came when Jack and his mother had no more money. Jack did not want to sell the pony and trap and the other things they had bought with the ogre's money; sooner than do that, he decided to pay a second visit to the tall house to see what he might find there. Of course, it would be dangerous, because no doubt the ogre's wife remembered his first visit and the lost bag of gold. Still, Jack was not the boy to mind a little danger. Indeed, he rather liked it, for life in his mother's cottage did not bring many adventures.

So stepping once more from the window one fine morning, he climbed the beanstalk ladder—up, up, and up, till he came to the broad white road on the far side of the clouds. Striding briskly along, he soon reached the ogre's house, and there was the tall woman at the door shaking out a mop.

'Good day to you, ma'am,' said Jack, 'and how are you this morning?'

'I was middling well till I seen you, young fellow-me-lad,' said the ogre's wife.

'Well, how about a bite of breakfast?'

'Last time I gave you a bite of breakfast,' said she, 'there was a bag of gold vanished from under my very nose.'

'You don't say so!' said Jack in a tone of great surprise. 'Now how could that have been?'

'Maybe you know more about it than I do,' said the ogre's wife.

'Well, maybe I do,' said Jack. 'And if you give me a bite of breakfast, I'll tell you all I know.'

The ogre's wife was very curious about the bag of gold, so she agreed to give Jack breakfast, and led the way into the kitchen. There she set before him some bread and cheese and a mug of milk.

When he had nearly fished it, there was a tremendous noise and the whole house shook. Thump, thump, thumpety thump! It was the ogre coming home for his breakfast.

'Into the oven with you,' said the ogre's wife, bundling Jack in and shutting the door after him. The door flew open with a bang, and the ogre came in. Two great oxen were hanging at his belt.

'Here, wife,' he said, throwing them down on the table. 'Cook me those for breakfast. But what's this I smell?

'Fee, fi, foh, fum!
I smell the blood of a British man.
Be he alive, or be he dead,
I'll grind his bones to make my bread!'

'Stuff and nonsense!' said his wife. 'It's last night's supper you're smelling—them two fat boys you had grilled on toast. Now sit down and rest yourself while I make your breakfast.'

After breakfast, the ogre said to his wife:

'Bring me my hen that lays the golden eggs.'

So the woman went out and brought in a fine grey-and-white speckled hen, and the ogre put it on the table and said, 'Lay!' Instantly the hen laid an egg of pure gold. It dropped on the table and rolled towards the edge, and the ogre caught it and put it in his pocket. Then he said 'Lay!' once more, and once more the hen dropped a golden egg on the kitchen table. But this time the ogre did not pocket it, for all of a sudden he felt sleepy after his night's work; his head fell forward and he began to snore. The noise was like the noise of twenty thunderstorms—so loud was it that it terrified Jack, even though he was inside the oven with a door of cast iron with knobs of solid brass.

As soon as her husband was asleep, the woman let Jack out of the oven, for she wanted to hear what he had to say about the stolen money-bag. Jack noticed the hen standing on the table with the golden egg beside it, and he thought it would be a useful hen to have. So he said to the ogre's wife:

'Just step outside and fetch me a mug of water from the pump, for being in the oven has made me mighty thirsty, and I can't tell you my tale with a dry throat.'

She did as she was bid, and instantly Jack took hold of the hen, tucked it under one arm, and ran out of doors. This alarmed the hen, which instantly set up a cackling.

The ogre jumped up from his sleep, seized his great holly club, and sprang out of doors after Jack. The ogre's wife, who was in the backyard, rushed in to see what had happened, but by this time Jack, the hen, and the ogre had all disappeared.

Jack tore down the road like the wind, with the ogre after him. The ogre had longer legs, but he was scarcely awake, and the breakfast he had eaten was still heavy inside him. Besides, Jack was nimble, and made the best of what start he had. Down the white road he ran, dodging and turning, with the grey hen under his arm flapping its wings and cackling as if to awaken the dead. The ogre pelted after him, swinging his great knobbly club and calling out in the most terrible language imaginable. The wind of his words seemed to drive Jack faster and faster forward, but the ogre was gaining on him. He was only a few yards behind. A terrible swing of his club nearly caught Jack full on the top of his head, but Jack dodged and flew on. Then something happened which saved him. A great cloud, bigger than all the others, rolled up from the side of the road and covered everything in a thick white mist. With a mighty effort Jack rushed forward and buried himself in the mist. He could only see the road for a few yards ahead. Plunging into a ditch by the roadside and lying there unseen, Jack waited till the ogre went thundering past, laying about him with the club and swearing horribly. A few minutes later, he came stumping back again, and Jack heard him mutter something about going home, for he had no luck that day. As soon as the ogre was out of earshot, Jack climbed out of the ditch and went on. In a few minutes, he had reached the beanstalk and was clambering down, the hen tucked safely under his arm. Down and down he went, until he came out of the cloud and could see his mother pottering about in the garden below.

'There!' he said, landing breathless at her feet and clutching the speckled hen. 'What do you think of this?'

'Lord-a-mercy!' said his mother. 'What will the boy be up to next?'

She followed the boy into the cottage, and he closed the door carefully behind her to make sure the hen did not escape. Then he set it down on the floor and told it to lay. The hen squatted down and in a few moments laid another perfect golden egg. The widow was full of amazement at the cleverness of her wonderful son. No sooner was the hen shut up securely in a wooden hutch than she put her shawl round her head and set off to town to buy the food they so sadly needed. And after that, whenever they wanted anything, they just told the speckled hen to lay an egg; and soon they were once more prosperous and happy.

4

At last Jack began to hanker after a little excitement. He decided to visit the ogre's house once more. Of course, he knew it would be dangerous, because now both the ogre and his wife would try to kill him. But he was not afraid, and one fine morning he stepped outside on to the beanstalk and began his upward climb. He climbed and he climbed and he climbed till he came to the broad white road. The sun was shining, and he felt light-hearted and careless. Nevertheless, when he got near the tall house, he advanced with care. There, sure enough, was the ogre's wife at the door. He waited till she disappeared, then he crept up to the door and looked cautiously inside. There was no one to be seen. The woman must be out in the backyard, or perhaps upstairs.

Jack slipped into the kitchen and looked round for some-where to hide. The woman would be sure to look in the oven; besides, a sizzling noise came out of it and it was very hot. Evidently there was something baking. So instead, Jack lifted the lid of the copper and looked inside. There was plenty of room. He climbed carefully in and lowered the lid.

He was not a moment too soon, for just then the ogre's wife came in, and in a few minutes there was a thump, thump, thumpety thump! and the ogre himself stalked in, shaking the whole house and calling for his breakfast. All at once he stopped and sniffed the air, very suspiciously.

'*Fee, fi, foh, fum!*'

he said in threatening tones,

> '*I smell the blood of a British man.*
> *Be he alive, or be he dead,*
> *I'll grind his bones to make my bread!*'

This time his wife did not say 'Nonsense!' She said, 'Now maybe you are right, husband, for I think I smell something myself.'

She went to the oven and opened it. Inside were three whole sheep roasting for the ogre's breakfast. And of course Jack was not there. She took out the sheep and set them on the table, and the ogre began his breakfast. Then she began look-ing round the room, under the chairs, in the cupboards, and even in the great chest where the ogre kept his money-bags.

'I can smell boy,' said the ogre.

'Depend upon it,' said his wife, 'it's that dratted child who stole the hen, and it's dearly I'd like to get my hands on the throat of him, so I would.'

And she went on searching, but she never thought of looking in the copper.

'There's not a sign of him,' said the ogre's wife at last.

'Well, I could have sworn I smelt boy,' said the ogre.

Then he finished his breakfast and began to feel sleepy, so he settled down in the rocking-chair and called for his magic harp. The woman brought out a little golden harp and put it on the table.

'Sing, harp,' said she, and at once the harp began to play and sing all by itself. Very strange and very beautiful were the songs it sang, until after a while the ogre fell asleep and the rumble of his snores reached Jack in the copper. Jack peeped out and saw that the ogre's wife had gone out of the room. He crept quietly out of the copper and seized the magic harp. No sooner had he done this than the harp made a great crashing chord and sang out loud and clear, 'Help, Master! Help, Master!' Jack ran out of the door clutching the harp, and the ogre sprang up, seized his holly club, and followed.

Down the broad white road ran Jack, and fortunately the ogre tripped on the doorstep in his haste to get out of the house. Cursing and swearing, he got up, rubbed his bruises, picked up his club, which had fallen from his hand, and began pounding along after Jack.

This time no kindly cloud rolled up to hide the boy, and although he twisted and turned to avoid his pursuer, the ogre gained on him steadily. And all the time the harp sounded its agonized cry, 'Master, Master, help me!'

Jack reached the beanstalk not a moment too soon. He began to climb down it like lightning, hardly stopping to put his feet on the steps made by the leaves. He almost slid down.

When he was halfway to the ground, the whole beanstalk shook as if it had been hit by a hurricane. Jack looked up for a moment and saw that the ogre had jumped on to the beanstalk and was climbing down after him. Madly, the beanstalk tottered and swayed under the ogre's weight, and every second brought him closer.

As he neared the ground Jack shouted:

'Mother, Mother, where are you? The axe! Fetch the axe!'

Just as Jack bumped to the ground, his mother came running out of the cottage with the new axe in her hand. There was a sudden shadow over the whole garden as the huge ogre came nearer and nearer. Jack swung the axe and brought it down with all his force on the twisted stem of the beanstalk. The whole mighty plant shook and swayed. One more blow and the stem was cut right through. With a horrible cry the ogre lost his hold and fell to the ground. He broke his neck and died instantly, and there was a great hole in the ground where he fell, which it took Jack three days to fill up again afterwards.

Well, that was the end of the magic beanstalk, and that was the end of the ogre too. As for his wife and the tall house, they were never heard of again, though I daresay they are still there at the end of the broad road above the clouds. Whenever the wind was fierce and strong, Jack used to tell his mother that it must be the ogre's wife moaning for the loss of her husband. But I daresay he was wrong, for it is well known that ogres' wives lose little time in getting themselves new husbands when anything happens to the old one.

Jack and his mother went on living happily in the little

cottage. Whenever they wanted money, they told the speckled hen to lay; and whenever they were dull, they told the magic harp to sing. Very strange and very wonderful were the songs it sang, so that they were never without company, for people came from near and far to listen.

TOM TIT TOT

———— ❖ ————

There was once a woman who baked five pies for dinner, and she left them in the oven too long. They were cooked quite hard, so that the knife would not cut them. She put them away on the shelf, saying they would come again. By this she meant that they would get soft, and could be eaten later. But her daughter Joan overheard her, and said to herself:

'Why, if they will come again, I may as well eat them.'

So being hungry she ate all the five pies, hard as they were, and very good she found them.

When supper-time came her mother said:

'Joan, go and fetch two or three of those pies.'

Joan went to the larder and looked on the shelf, but of course they were not there.

'They haven't come again yet,' said she to her mother, 'so you can't have them.'

'Not come yet?' said her mother. 'Fetch one of them, and let's have a look.'

'I can't fetch one,' said Joan, 'for not even one of them has come again. I ate them all, and I ought to know.'

'You've eaten all the five pies?' asked her mother in surprise. 'What a wonderful fine appetite you have, to be sure.'

As there were no pies for supper, she went and sat in the doorway and began spinning. And as she spun, she sang to herself, and this is what she sang:

> *'My daughter has eaten five—*
> *Five pies today.'*

Now it happened that the King was passing down the street at that moment, and he heard the woman singing, so he said:

'What song is that you are singing, ma'am?'

The woman did not like to tell the King the real words, because she did not want him to think her daughter was greedy, so she changed the words.

'"My daughter has spun five—five skeins today." Those are the words I was singing, Your Majesty.'

With that the woman rose from her stool and made the King a curtsy.

'Indeed?' said the King. 'What a wonderful spinner your daughter is! I should like to see her.'

The woman brought out her daughter, and the King said:

'It happens that I am looking for a wife. You seem a likely girl, as well as a wonderful spinner. How would you like to marry me and be Queen?'

'I should like it very much, Your Majesty,' said Joan, and made a deep curtsy.

'Very well,' said the King. 'I will marry you, and for eleven months of the year you may have fine clothes and all the money you want, all the food you need, and whatever company you like. But for the twelfth month of the year you must spin me five skeins of flaxen thread every day. What do you say?'

Now Joan and her mother knew very well that she could never spin five skeins a day, for that is a very great deal, even for a practised spinner; but they thought that when the time came, some way out of the difficulty could be found. So they told the King they were willing for him to marry Joan on those conditions.

Joan and the King were married, and there was a magnificent ceremony, and for the first few months everything went well. Joan had all the food she wanted, money and fine clothes, and whatever company she liked; though the company she liked best was that of the King himself, for as the months went on, she loved him more and more dearly. The eleven months went all too quickly, but Joan hoped that the King had forgotten all about the five skeins a day she had promised to spin during the last month. However, when the last day of the eleventh month came, he took her up to a room at the top of the castle, where she had never been before. In it there was nothing but a spinning-wheel, a stool, a bare table, and a bed for her to lie on.

'This is where you must stay for a whole month,' he said. 'Every morning I shall bring you your breakfast and the flax to spin, and every evening I shall bring you your supper and take away the five skeins of yarn you have spun during the day. But the very first time you fail to spin the five skeins, next day your head will be cut off.'

As soon as poor Joan was left to herself, she sat down on the stool and began to cry. However was she to spin *one* skein of flax in a day, let alone five? She was a clumsy girl with her hands, and had never learnt to use a spinning-wheel. The King would bring her the flax and return for the skeins of yarn in the evening, and he would discover she was no spinner at all, so her head would be cut off, and that would be the end of her marriage and her life as well.

Then as she sat crying, Joan heard a little sound of knocking at the door, and she said, 'Come in,' and into the room came a small black thing with very bright eyes, twitching pointed ears, and a long tail. He looked at Joan out of the corners of his eyes and said:

'What's the matter here?'

'That's nothing to you,' answered Joan.

'Maybe it is, and maybe it isn't,' That said. 'Tell me what it is, and I shall know.'

So Joan told him all about the burnt pies and her marriage to the King and the five skeins of flax that she had to spin or have her head cut off.

'Well, I can help you,' That said. 'Every morning when you get the flax, I will come along and take it away with me, and in the evening I will bring it back, spun into five skeins.'

'I see,' said Joan, 'and what is your price?'

'Every day I will give you three guesses,' said the little black thing, 'and you just guess my name. If you don't guess it by the time the month is up, I shall have you for myself.'

'All right,' said Joan, 'it's a bargain.'

What else could she do? She knew she could never spin the flax herself, and if nobody helped her, she would certainly lose her head. Besides, she was sure she could think of the name of the little black thing before the end of the month. Without further words, That twirled That's tail, rose up in the air, and flew out of the window.

Next morning the King brought Joan her breakfast and the

flax to spin and left her to herself. No sooner had he gone than That came flying in and took away the flax. So Joan spent the day thinking of names that That might be called.

Just as darkness was falling, in flew the black thing with the five skeins of flax, and very skilfully they had been spun.

'Now,' said he, 'what's my name? You have three guesses.'

'Might it be Bill?' said Joan.

That twirled That's tail and said: 'No, it mightn't.'

'Might it be Ned?' asked Joan.

That laughed.

'No,' That said. 'It might not neither.'

'Then maybe it is Mark,' said Joan.

That twirled That's tail and laughed again.

'That it might not,' That said, and flew off out of the window.

Presently the King came in with some supper, and he was mighty pleased when he saw the five skeins of flax.

'Well, my dear,' he said, 'you won't have to be beheaded tomorrow, I see.'

Next day the King brought more flax, and That came and took it away and brought it back in the evening, and asked Joan what his name was. Every day the same thing happened, but still Joan could not guess his name. She tried everything she knew—names of the boys she had known at home, names from storybooks, and names from the Bible. And the nearer and nearer came the end of the month, the more gleeful and malicious That grew, twirling his tail and rolling his little fiery eyes.

On the last day but one, he brought the finished skeins as usual, and as usual he said, 'What's my name?'

'Happen it's Nicodemus,' said Joan.

127

'Happen it's not then,' said the little imp, laughing spite-fully. 'What next?'

'Then maybe it's Sammle,' said Joan.

'And maybe it isn't,' said the imp, twirling his tail fiercely.

'Then it must be Methusalem,' said Joan, almost in despair.

'That it's not,' said he with a terrible laugh. 'There's only one more day, my girl, and you shall be mine!'

And That twirled That's tail so maliciously that it could scarce be seen, and glared at Joan out of his fiery eyes till she felt terribly frightened. Then off he flew.

Poor Joan was in a bad way, but the King, when he came in with supper and the last of the flax, looked more pleased than ever.

'I don't doubt, my dear,' he said, 'that you'll spin the five skeins tomorrow just as you have spun them every day before; so to show how happy I am that your life will be spared, I have brought my own supper and will sit and eat it with you.'

Never a word said Joan about the little black imp, and together they ate their supper. Hardly had the King eaten a mouthful when he burst out laughing.

'What is there to be so happy about?' asked Joan.

'Why, my dear,' answered the King, 'I almost forgot to tell you. The funniest thing happened today when I was out hunt-ing. We got to the edge of a wood, and down at the bottom of an old chalk-pit was sitting a little black creature with a twirling tail. He was sitting on a stool spinning away at a small spinning-wheel. It was turning away as fast as fast, and as it turned the black creature sang. This is what it sang, and I can't make head nor tail of it.

> *"Nimmy nimmy not—*
> *My name is TOM TIT TOT!"*

Now what do you make of that, my dear?'

Joan's heart was leaping for joy, but she said nothing. When the King had gone, she repeated the rhyme to herself over and over again to make sure she remembered it right, and after that she fell asleep.

Next evening, That brought back the finished skeins just as before, and this time he was looking more crafty and gleeful than ever. He gave her the skeins and asked:

'What is my name?'

Joan pretended to be frightened.

'Might it be—Solomon?' she asked.

'Try again!' shouted the imp, grinning horribly, and coming farther into the room.

Joan hesitated, and paused as if she were thinking desperately.

'Then it must be Zebedee,' she said faintly.

'Not that neither!' shouted the imp with a devilish laugh, coming still closer to Joan and holding out his little black hands towards her. 'One more guess, my little one, and then you are mine!'

Joan shrank back into a corner of the room as if she were dreadfully frightened, and at last she pointed a finger at the little black demon, and said with a joyful laugh:

> 'Nimmy nimmy not—
> Your name is TOM TIT TOT!'

Instantly there was a flash of lightning, a clap of thunder; Tom Tit Tot gave a great cry, twirled his tail in spite and anger, and flew out of the window, his eyes blazing like coals of fire. And that was the end of That—for Joan never saw him again. When the King came in, he brought Joan no supper—instead, he took one look at the five finished skeins, and led Joan downstairs to feast with him in his own hall.

THE GOLDEN SNUFF-BOX

O nce upon a time—and a very good time it was, though it was neither in your time, nor in my time, nor in anyone else's time—there lived a poor woodcutter and his wife in the middle of a dark forest, and they had one son named Jack. Now Jack had never seen anybody else in the world, for he had not set foot outside the forest; but he knew there were other people besides himself and his mother and father, because he had read about them in books. So one day, while his father was out cutting wood, he said to his mother:

'If I stay here in the forest, Mother, I shall never learn anything. I want to go out into the world by myself and see other lands and other people. Will you let me go and seek my fortune?'

'Why, yes,' said Jack's mother. 'I am an old woman, but I have your father still; and so long as we have each other, we shall not be lonely without you. I will give you something to eat, and you shall go right away. Would you rather have a small cake with my blessing or a big cake with my curse?'

'Oh, give me the big cake!' cried Jack. 'I have far to go, and I may be hungry on the road.'

So the old woman said goodbye to her son, and gave him a big cake wrapped up in a cloth. As soon as he had gone, she climbed to the top of the house, and cursed him until he was out of sight. She called him a wicked boy for leaving his old mother, and wished him ill fortune and great hardship.

After a while Jack came upon his father chopping the branches off a tree he had just felled.

'Where are you off to, son?' asked the woodcutter.

Jack told him the same as he had told his mother, and asked his father to bid him farewell and give him his blessing. The woodcutter answered by fumbling in a pocket of his waistcoat. Presently he pulled out a little gold snuff-box, which he held out to Jack between his forefinger and thumb.

'Here,' he said, 'take this. Keep it with you wherever you go, and do not open the lid until you are near death.'

Jack took the box, put it in his pocket, and thanked his father. Then he bade him goodbye, and his father wished him luck. He strode along the path, and soon he could not even hear the strokes of the woodcutter's axe.

On and on Jack went, up hills, down valleys, through woodland and marshland, across rivers and streams. At last night fell. He was hungry and tired, for he had travelled many miles and eaten all the cake his mother had given him. He looked round for somewhere to pass the night. In the distance he saw a light from a window. He trudged wearily towards it, and found it came from a fine house belonging to some gentleman. He knocked at the back door, and a servant answered him. He asked her for some food, and some straw to sleep on for the night. She told him to sit down at the kitchen table, and got him food and drink in plenty.

While he was eating, a girl came and looked at him. It was the gentleman's daughter. Jack had never seen a young lady before, and he thought he had never seen anything so pretty in his whole life. As for the girl, she ran upstairs and told her father who was in the kitchen.

'Father,' cried Maria, for that was the girl's name, 'there is a handsome, bright young fellow downstairs in the kitchen. He says his name is Jack, and he is off to seek his fortune.'

'Oh indeed, daughter,' answered the gentleman. 'Let us have him up here and see what he is like.'

So Maria went down to the kitchen and asked Jack to step up and speak to her father.

'If you want to stay here, young fellow,' said the gentleman, 'you must work.'

'Why yes, sir,' said Jack, 'that will I do very willingly.'

'What can you do?' asked the gentleman.

'Anything,' said Jack, meaning that he could turn his hand to any odd job that was to be done about the house.

But the gentleman chose to understand him differently.

'Anything!' he repeated. 'Anything! Well, if you can do anything, I'll tell you what you must do. First thing tomorrow morning, you must make me a huge lake in my park with a great sailing-vessel on it, a man-of-war; and exactly at eight o'clock it must fire a royal salute with its big gun, and the noise of the gun must be so terrible and loud that it breaks a leg of the bed where my daughter Maria is asleep. Can you do that?'

'I don't know,' said Jack; but the gentleman looked so stern and fierce that he added, 'but I will do my best, sir, indeed I will.'

'That you had better,' said the gentleman, 'otherwise you shall be put to death! No more words; goodnight, and get you to bed.'

Jack wished Maria and her father goodnight, and the servant took him to the room where he was to pass the night. Poor Jack hardly had time to wonder how he was to get out of his difficulties before sleep overcame him. So weary he was with his long day's tramp that he slept as sound as a log till morning.

2

So soundly did Jack sleep that he did not wake up until nearly eight o'clock. Suddenly he remembered that he had to make a lake in the gentleman's park, with a man-of-war on it, and that the man-of-war had to fire a royal salute so loud that it broke the leg of the young lady's bed. Poor Jack! He knew he could not possibly perform the task, and he began to wonder how the gentleman would put him to death. He hoped it would not be too painful and long drawn-out. Then, all at once he remembered his father's gold snuff-box. Quickly taking it out of his pocket, he opened the lid. Out jumped three little red men, who stood on the table bowing to him.

'Here we are,' said one of them, 'all ready to do your bidding. What would you have us do?'

Jack told them the task he had to perform.

'Have no fear,' said the little red man. 'It shall be done instantly.'

At that they all disappeared. Jack went quickly to the window and looked out across the park. Already one of the meadows was covered with water. It grew deeper and deeper.

Presently there was an immense sheet of water, which rapidly became a lake. In the very centre of it floated a warship. Its sails were furled, but Jack could see the mouths of the great cannon. It was a minute to eight o'clock. All at once there was a deafening roar from the warship, and a flash of fire from the biggest of the guns. A cloud of smoke rose above the lake. Then just as the clock over the gentleman's stable was striking eight, the gun roared out for the last time in a deafening explosion.

Maria, only just waking from sleep, was suddenly jerked out of bed by the gun's report, which was so loud that it broke one of the legs of her bed.

She ran to her father, who was already up. He was gazing with delight at the huge lake in his grounds and the man-of-war floating in the centre of it.

'Well,' he said, 'your young fellow is not such a fool as he looks.'

'He is as clever as he is handsome,' agreed Maria.

Just then Jack came in, and Maria and her father both congratulated him and told him how clever he was.

'Now,' said the gentleman, 'since you are so clever, there is one more thing I would like you to do for me, and if you succeed, I will give you my daughter in marriage. How would you like that?'

Jack looked at the young lady and she smiled, and the young lady looked at Jack and he smiled, and they both agreed that it would be a very good marriage.

'Don't be too sure of yourselves,' said the gentleman. 'This is a much harder task than the last one. I have always had a mind to have a great castle, and this is what I want you to build for me. You see that grove of trees over there at the top of the hillside? Well, tomorrow morning, by eight o'clock, the whole of that grove is to be cut down, and there must be a fine castle in its place, standing on twelve gold pillars. And the courtyard is to be filled with soldiers, and just at eight o'clock, their officer is to appear before them on a white horse and order them to present arms. If everything is done as I have described it, you shall have my daughter in marriage. But if you fail, your life shall be forfeit.'

So Jack told the gentleman he would do his best, though he was afraid the task might be beyond the powers even of the little men in the snuff-box.

Next morning, he woke up a little before eight, and remembering what he had to do, he took the snuff-box out of his pocket, where he always kept it for safety, and opened the lid. Just as before, the three little men hopped out and asked him his will. Jack told them exactly what was needed, and hardly had he finished speaking before they had all three vanished. Jack got dressed and went downstairs. Maria and her father were already looking out of the window towards the grove of trees. And already they could hear the sound of axes falling upon trunks, though there was never a woodcutter to be seen. However, Jack, who had seen his father cut down many a tall forest tree, could tell that the work was being done expertly. Presently there was not a tree on the hillside; and in a few minutes, a wonderful castle had arisen on twelve pillars of solid gold.

Never had there been such a castle! The walls and turrets were of fine white stone, the windows were shapely and numerous, the battlements and towers strong and fair to see.

Just before eight o'clock, the three of them walked through the park to see the castle at close quarters; and as they did so, they noticed that the courtyard was filled with soldiers in smart uniforms, drilling, marching, and forming fours. Then as the clock in the great tower began to strike the hour, an officer on a splendid white horse rode out in front of the soldiers and ordered them to present arms. This they all did with the smartness and precision of the King's own guards.

The gentleman was delighted. What a splendid castle, and what fine soldiers! He was tremendously proud of Jack and very eager to have him as a son-in-law. As for Maria, she was a happy as a thousand sunbeams. Then the gentleman sent messengers all over the countryside to summon the nobility and gentry to a hunting party, so that they could inspect the castle and the lake with the warship on it.

By dinner-time a great assembly had collected round the gentleman's house, and already some of them had begun to ask whom the fine castle belonged to. But the gentleman said nothing, for he planned to take them hunting first, and afterwards to lead them round the castle. So as soon as everyone was ready, the hounds were loosed from the kennels and the hunt began. Everyone went—Jack and Maria as well as the gentleman himself, and all his friends and neighbours.

But a very unfortunate thing befell. Jack had left his snuff-box behind when he had changed to go hunting; and the manservant who had helped him dress had found it in his waistcoat pocket. This manservant, seeing that everyone was out of the way, walked over to the castle with the box in his pocket; and when he was inside the castle, he took it out and opened the lid. Instantly the three red men appeared and asked the servant what his will was.

'Why,' said he, 'I should like you to carry this whole castle, with me inside it, far away to a distant country.' Almost before he had finished speaking, the castle rose in the air and was whirled away out of sight. So that when the hunting party returned towards evening, there was no castle to be seen.

The gentleman was furious with Jack.

'This is some trick of yours,' he said. 'I don't believe there was ever a castle there at all! You shall never set eyes on my daughter again, for I shall have you put to death instantly.'

But Jack and Maria both pleaded with him, until at last he relented and said he would pardon Jack, provided he could find the castle and bring it back to him within a year and a day.

Jack agreed to this though he had not the least idea how to set about finding the castle, for he had lost the snuff-box and did not know where to turn for help. But he said he would do his best; then bidding Maria a sorrowful farewell, he set off upon the very horse on which he had been out hunting.

3

For days and days Jack travelled the world in search of the lost castle on twelve golden pillars, and he had never a sight of it. For weeks and weeks he rode on, for months and months, until his year and a day were almost gone. He began to think he would never find it.

One day he reached a great palace, and it turned out to be the palace of the King of All the Mice. He rode up to the gate, where a single mouse stood on sentry-go. The mouse asked Jack who he was and what was his business, and Jack told him he wanted to speak to the King. So another mouse took him into the royal presence, and the King of All the Mice asked him what he wanted.

Jack told him, and the King said he was sorry and would do all he could to help.

'In the morning,' he said, 'I will call up all the mice in the world and find out if any of them has seen this castle.'

After that Jack was given supper; and next morning, when he woke up, he saw out of the window a great host of mice, thousands and thousands of twirling whiskers and twisting tails and little black, glinting eyes. Then a trumpet was sounded and a herald made a proclamation; and the proclamation said that if any mouse had seen a castle on twelve golden pillars anywhere in the world, he was to come at once into the presence of the King. But not a mouse stirred. Not one mouse in all that company had set eyes on the castle.

So when they had all gone, the King called to Jack and told him that he had two brothers—the King of All the Frogs and the King of All the Birds, and Jack had better go and visit them, for perhaps they could help him.

'Leave your horse here,' said the King of All the Mice, 'and I will lend you a fresh one. Take this cake to my brother the Frog King, and tell him I am well. He will know by the cake that you come from me.'

So Jack mounted a fresh horse, put the cake in his saddle-bag, thanked the Mouse King for his kindness, and rode out at the palace gate. At the gate he was stopped by the sentry, who asked Jack if he would like him to go along with him. Jack could not think what use a mouse would be to him, but he said the sentry could come if he liked. So the mouse ran nimbly up the horse's leg, and this tickled the horse and away he sped. Jack put the mouse safely in his pocket and forgot all about him.

On and on they rode till they came to the palace of the King of All the Frogs. At the gate there was a frog on sentry-go, who challenged Jack, and when Jack told him he wanted to speak to the King, he called up a frog messenger who led him into the royal presence.

The Frog King thanked Jack for the good news of his brother, the Mouse King, and for the cake which he had brought. But he told Jack that he had no idea where the lost castle was.

'But,' said the Frog King, 'stay here the night, and in the morning I will call up all the frogs in the world, and surely one or other of them will have some idea where the castle is.'

Next morning Jack was awakened by a great croaking. Never had he heard such a croaking! And he looked out of the window and saw the palace was surrounded by a huge throng of frogs, all gazing up at the palace with great goggle eyes. A frog trumpeter blew a loud blast, and a frog herald read out a proclamation. Then all the frogs looked at one another with their goggle eyes and gulped a few times, but none came forward to say he had seen the castle on golden pillars.

So the King dismissed the frogs, and they all went hopping off to the ends of the earth; and when they had gone, the Frog King told Jack he had better go and ask his brother the King of All the Birds.

'Take a fresh horse,' he said, 'and deliver this cake to my brother. Say I am in good health, and ask the Bird King to help you because you have been a guest of mine.'

Jack thanked the King of the Frogs, took the cake, mounted

his horse, and rode away. And as he reached the palace gate, the sentry stopped him and asked him if he would like a companion on his way. Jack could not see what use a frog would be, but he said he could go with him if he liked. So the frog sentry hopped up, and Jack put him in his pocket and forgot all about him.

Away they rode, and soon the palace of the Frog King was left far behind. Over rivers and mountains they sped, until at last they came to the palace of the King of All the Birds. At the gateway there was a bird sentry. Jack told him he wanted to speak to the King, as he had a message for him from his brother the Frog King. So the sentry called up a bird messenger, who brought Jack into the presence of the King. Jack gave him the cake, and told him his brother was in good health and desired that he would help him to find the castle on golden pillars.

'I am glad my brother is well,' said the Bird King, 'and I rejoice to receive this present. I will do all I can to help you. My subjects the birds range far and wide over the whole world, and surely one of them will have seen this castle. Tomorrow I will call them all together and make inquiries. In the meanwhile, eat, drink, and be merry, so far as my poor hospitality will allow.'

Next morning Jack awoke to the sound of a million birds. There they were, all the birds in the world, fluttering, chirping, and chattering together—all except *one*. A trumpet was sounded, and the King came out on to the balcony of his palace.

'Where is the Great Bird?' he demanded in shrill but stern tones.

No one had seen him. The King signalled to two small birds who were hovering nearby.

'Call down the Great Bird,' the King commanded, 'and tell him we are all waiting for him.'

So the two little birds flew off. Up and up they went until they were out of sight; and soon they returned leading a great, fierce eagle. He flew down on his broad wings and alighted on a pinnacle of the King's palace. Then all the birds were silent, and the herald proclaimed the proclamation.

'Whereas,' called the herald, 'the friend of the King of All the Fowls of the Air has lost, misplaced, and mislaid a great and mighty castle which stands upon twelve legs or pillars of solid gold, being the possession of his father-in-law to be, a gentleman of the county of Such-and-So, it is hereby commanded that if any of the fowls of the air has seen the aforesaid castle, he is to proclaim the same instantly or forever hold his peace!'

Then all the birds looked at one another, and the King called, loud and shrill:

'Have any of you seen the castle?'

The eagle flapped his wings, raised his head, and opened his great beak.

'Yes!' he said proudly. '*I* have seen it.'

4

At this news there was great rejoicing. Never did you hear such a cawing and a chirruping and a fluting as was set up that instant all round the palace of the Bird King. The King called the eagle to him, and when the noise had died down and the other birds had flown away, he told him to take Jack instantly to the place where he had seen the castle.

Jack, you may be sure, was overjoyed, for he was thinking of getting back to Maria, whom he had not seen for nearly a year. And he thanked the King of the Birds profusely, and the King bade him farewell and commanded the eagle to make good speed. So the eagle spread his wings, and Jack climbed up between them. Soon they were aloft over the palace, and before long the palace was no more to be seen.

Away they flew over pine-woods and mountains, rivers and lakes, sometimes to be lost in the clouds, sometimes to be borne swiftly upon the wind—until at length they came within sight of the castle. There it was, standing upon its twelve gold pillars amid a group of pleasant green hills.

They alighted on the top of a nearby oak tree, and Jack began to consider how to get the castle back to his master, the gentleman. The first thing to be done was to get back the gold snuff-box, since without the help of the little red men, he could never transport the castle.

All at once he remembered the mouse in his pocket. He took him out and told him to go and find the snuff-box if he could. The mouse sped down the oak tree and into the castle. Jack did not have to wait long. Presently the mouse returned with the box firmly between his forepaws.

'We had better fly off and find the gentleman and tell him that his castle is found,' said Jack. 'That is the first thing to do.'

So away they flew, until there was no more land in sight, for they were over the Great Sea. Not an inch of dry ground was to be seen. But alas!, while they were flying over the sea, the mouse and the frog fell to quarrelling about which should carry the snuff-box, so that the box slipped out of their grasp and fell into the water, miles below.

'Quickly!' cried Jack to the eagle. 'Fly down, for we must find it at all costs. Without it, I am lost.'

So the eagle swooped down like a thunderbolt until he was hovering only a short way above the blue water.

'This is where I can be useful,' said the frog; and with a croak, he jumped off the eagle's back and dived into the sea. Three days and nights he was under the water, but at last he came to the surface with the snuff-box safe between his jaws. Once more, Jack and the frog and the mouse were all on the eagle's back, with the snuff-box in the pocket of Jack's coat.

Over deserts and plains they flew, over forests and hills, until they came to the palace of the King of All the Birds. Here Jack thanked the eagle for his kindness, and asked the King if he could have his horse to take back to the King of the Frogs. He had no time to lose, for the year was almost at an end. Mounting the horse, he galloped away until he came to the palace of the Frog King.

Jack told him his brother the Bird King was well, and asked him if he could change his horse for the horse belonging to the Mouse King. He thanked the frog for his services, and the frog hopped away into the bulrushes to tell his friends of his adventures. Then Jack bade farewell for the last time to the Frog King and galloped off to the palace of the Mouse King. The mouse sentry was in one pocket and the snuff-box in the other.

When he reached the palace of the Mouse King, he thanked the mouse sentry for his help, and asked the King if he could change his horse for the horse on which he had arrived. He told him that his brothers were both well, and then galloped away at full speed, for it was the very last day of the year. Off they went, thundering through woods and valleys, until at length they came within reach of the country where the gentleman lived with his daughter. They had to travel at a tremendous speed, not even stopping when night fell, for they had many, many miles to go. Luckily the moon was full that night. Luckily, too, the horse was one of the strongest and swiftest horses in the world, otherwise they would never have arrived in time. Next morning Maria was sitting anxiously beside her window at home. For a whole year she had waited for a sign of Jack and the great castle, but not a word of news had come. Her father was impatient and angry. A year had passed, and now there was no hope.

'You were a fool,' he said, 'ever to talk to such an idiot. No good has he brought us; instead, nothing but disappointment and mockery.'

'A year and a day have not quite passed,' said Maria, though indeed she had little hope. Then all at once she heard something. It was the sound of a horse's hooves, and it came from beyond the park. In a few moments the horse galloped into sight, and a little later Jack stood breathless in front of her and her father.

'Oh, how glad I am to see you back,' said Maria; but her father was frowning.

'A year ago,' he said, 'I spared your life on condition that you restored my castle. It has disappeared, and I have become the laughing-stock of the whole county. Where is my castle?'

'The time is not quite up,' said Jack. 'I have ridden day and night to get back in time, and now I am weary. I beg you, sir, go and order your cook to prepare me some food, and afterwards, if I can bring it about, you shall have your castle.'

Well, there is no need to tell all that happened during the rest of that day. Before evening, Jack opened the snuff-box and ordered the three little men to fetch the castle; and before long, there it was on its twelve gold pillars, with the lights from its windows shining in the lake. And to make a long story short, Maria and Jack were married, and a splendid feast was held in the castle for all the nobility and gentry. The serving-man who had taken the snuff-box on the day of the hunt was told to go and get himself employment somewhere else.

The feast at the castle was followed by a magnificent ball, and the fame of the gentleman spread far and wide until it came to the ears of the King himself, so that the gentleman was made into a lord, and very proud and grand he became. As for his daughter, Maria, and Jack, the woodcutter's son, for all I know, they lived happily ever afterwards.

THE STARS IN THE SKY

———— ❖ ————

O nce upon a time, there was a little girl who wanted to reach the stars in the sky. She saw them shining on clear nights through the panes of her window, and she thought how happy she would be if only she could reach them. She asked her father and her mother if they could get them for her, and they only told her not to be silly. So she would fall asleep thinking how much she would like to have the stars, all the same.

One day she set off by herself to find them. First, she came to an old mill beside a mill-pond; and she said to the mill-pond, 'If you please, have you seen the stars in the sky?'

'Why, yes,' answered the mill-pond, 'they often come and play in my water. Jump in and swim, and perhaps you will find them.'

So the little girl jumped into the mill-pond, and she swam and she swam and she swam, but still she could not find them. All she could find was a little brook, so she asked the brook:

'Have you seen the stars in the sky? I would very much like to reach them.'

'Why, yes,' answered the brook, 'they often come down

and play on my banks. Paddle along, and perhaps you will find them.'

So she paddled and she paddled and she paddled, till she got tired, but still she could not find the stars in the sky. Instead, she came to a meadow where the fairies were playing.

'If you please,' she asked of the fairies, 'have you seen the stars in the sky? I would very much like to know where I can find them.'

'Why, yes,' said the fairies, 'they often shine in the grass at our feet. Dance with us and perhaps you will find them.'

So the little girl danced, and she danced, and she danced, but still she could not find them. She was by now very, very tired, so she sat down and cried.

'I've swum, and I've paddled, and I've danced,' she said, 'and still I haven't found the stars. If you can't help me then nobody can.'

'Little girl,' said the fairies, 'if you will not go home to your mother, then go forward.'

'Shall I reach the stars in the sky?' she asked.

'Perhaps,' said the fairies. 'You must ask four feet to carry two feet to no feet at all, and no feet at all will carry you to the stair with no steps; and if you climb the stair with no steps, either you will be near the stars in the sky or you will be somewhere else.'

So she thanked the fairies, and said goodbye, and set off with fresh courage, trying to remember what they had said.

Presently she came to a dark forest, and, tied to a tree at the edge of it, stood a horse.

'If you please,' said the little girl to the horse, 'can you help me to find the stars in the sky?'

'No,' said the horse, 'that has nothing to do with me. My business is to serve the fairies.'

'It was the fairies who told me to ask four feet to carry two feet to no feet at all, and no feet should carry me to the stair without steps, and if I could climb that, I might reach the stars.'

'If that is so,' said the horse, 'untie the rope and jump on my back.'

So the little girl did as she was told, and instantly the horse started off through the dark forest. Before long, they had gone right through the forest and reached a broad road; and the broad road took them to the sea, and there the horse stopped.

'Get off my back, little girl,' said the horse, 'for I have done what the fairies ordered.'

She jumped down from the horse's back and said:

'If you please, can you help me to find no feet at all?'

'That is none of my business,' answered the horse. 'I have brought you to the edge of the land, and that is as far as four feet can go.'

So saying, he threw up his head, turned round, and galloped off towards the dark forest, leaving the little girl standing beside the sea.

Just as she was wondering what to do next, a great and strange fish appeared at her feet and put its head out of the water.

'If you please,' said the little girl, 'can you help me to find the stars in the sky?'

'No,' said the fish, 'that is none of my business. My business is to serve the fairies.'

'It was the fairies,' she answered, 'who told me to find no

feet, who should take me to the stair without steps, and if I climbed them I might find the stars.'

'If that is so,' said the great and strange fish, 'jump on my back.'

So she jumped on the fish's back and sat astride, and this was no easy task, for the fish was slippery, but she took hold of one of its fins, and away they went.

They swam across the sea on a wide, shining track of light, at the end of which was a thing in the sky; and the thing was of many colours, red and yellow, blue and green, and it stretched right across the sky. At last they reached the bottom of the thing, and the fish said:

'Now you must get off my back, little girl; I have brought you to the stair with no steps, and there I must leave you, for I have done as the fairies ordered.'

So the little girl slid off the fish's back, and it turned round, and away it swam and was soon out of sight.

The little girl stood alone at the bottom of the thing in the sky, and she was very much afraid because she was so small and the stair was so steep; but she was full of wonder because the thing was so bright and radiant. So she began to climb. She climbed and she climbed and she climbed, but still she did not reach the stars in the sky. And the higher she got, the brighter grew the light, till she began to feel giddy. Dizzier and dizzier she grew, until suddenly she slipped and fell. Down, down, down she dropped, and might have been falling to this day, had she not struck the floor in her own bedroom, and woken up and found that it was morning.

MOLLY WHIPPLE

— ❖ —

There was once a poor couple who lived in a little house with their sons and daughters. They had so many children that they were at their wits' end to know how to feed and clothe them. Every day they seemed to be in need of more and more money, but the man could not work hard enough to earn more; as for his wife, she was at it from morning till night, cooking and sewing, cleaning and mending. At last there was only one thing to do. They went off into the woods with their three youngest children and left them there. The hearts of the poor couple were heavy, for they did not want to part with the three girls, but they feared that if they did not do so, the others might starve.

The three little girls walked on and on in search of food and shelter, and at last they came to a house at the edge of the wood. Darkness was beginning to fall, and there was a light in the window. They knocked at the door, and a woman opened it.

'Can you give us some supper?' they asked. 'We have lost our home and are hungry.'

'I can't do that, my dears,' said the woman. 'My husband is

a great giant, and if he comes home and finds you, he'll kill you, and perhaps eat you whole for his supper.'

'Oh, please,' said the eldest of the three girls in a very small voice, 'we're not afraid. Don't you think you could give us just a little supper? We're *so* tired and hungry.'

And she began to cry.

Then the giant's wife thought to herself that, after all, it might not be a bad idea to keep the three girls for the night—perhaps her husband would be glad of a change from his usual mutton and beef and pork. So she said:

'Well, come in, my dears, and I'll give you some bread and milk, and you shall sit by the fire and get warm.'

So they thanked her and went inside, though none of them much liked the idea of having supper with a giant's wife. But she did them no harm, and after eating they felt better, and were just thinking of going off to find somewhere to sleep when there was a great tramping of boots and the giant returned. The little girls were so frightened that they trembled in their shoes, but the giant's wife told them not to be alarmed.

'Come,' she said, 'hide in this cupboard till he's had his supper. Then perhaps he won't find you.'

And she pushed them all three into a great, dark cupboard.

The giant strode into the room, threw down his great club, and smelt the air.

'*Fee, fi, foh, fum,*'

said he,

'*I smell the blood of some earthly one.*'

'Stuff!' said his wife. 'You're always smelling things. Sit

152

down like a good boy and have your supper, and afterwards you shall see what a surprise I have for you.'

After supper she flung open the door of the cupboard and brought out the three girls.

'Here are three nice little girls,' she said. 'I have given them supper, and now they are going to stay the night. They can get into the same bed as our own three daughters. It'll be rather a squash, but they must manage as best they can.'

So the three little girls went to bed with the giant's three daughters, and how those daughters snored and snuffed in their sleep!

Now the youngest of the three little girls was very smart and clever, and her name was Molly Whipple. She had noticed with her sharp eyes that just before he had come and taken away the candle and bidden his daughters good night, the giant had put three necklaces of gold on their necks. But the necklaces he had put on Molly and her two sisters were of rope. So Molly, tired as she was, managed to stay awake till everyone else was sleeping soundly, and the giant's three daughters were snoring their heads off. Then she quickly took the necklaces of rope from her own and her sisters' necks and put them on the giant's daughters instead of the gold necklaces. These she put on herself and her sisters.

In the dead of night, the giant came stalking into the room with his club in his hand. He felt for the necks of the three girls with rope necklaces on, dragged them out of bed and beat them to death with his club. Then he gave a horrible laugh and stalked out.

The two sisters of Molly Whipple awoke crying, but Molly told them to be quiet and get up, for they must leave the

153

house before the giant or his wife awoke. So very early, when it was hardly morning, they crept out of the door and made off as fast as they could.

When morning came, they reached the palace of the King. Molly led her sisters boldly up to the gate and asked to be taken to the King.

'Who are you?' asked His Majesty when he saw them.

'We are three poor sisters,' said Molly, 'and we have just escaped from a cruel giant. If I may say so, Your Majesty, you ought not to allow such a dreadful creature to live in your kingdom.'

'That is easily said,' answered the King. 'Perhaps you will tell me how I can get rid of him?'

'Well,' said Molly Whipple, 'you must first get his sword.'

'Would you like to get it for me, young lady?' asked the King.

'I can try, Your Majesty,' said Molly. 'What will you do for me if I get the giant's sword?'

'I will promise my eldest son to your eldest sister,' said the King.

'It's a bargain, Your Majesty,' said Molly; and after that they were all given a meal in the royal palace.

That evening, Molly returned alone to the giant's house, and when it was dark, she slipped in unseen and hid under the giant's bed; for she saw that his great sword hung at the bed's head. Presently he came thumping in from his supper, sniffed a little, but was too sleepy to look under the bed, and was soon snoring so that the whole room shook and the banging of the bed nearly drove Molly deaf. Then she crept out and seized hold of the sword, which was hanging behind the giant's head.

As she crept towards the door with it, she found it so heavy that she could not help rattling it against the floor; and the noise woke the giant, who instantly sprang out of bed, and without waiting to pick up his club, gave a great roar and followed Molly out of the cottage. He took long strides, but Molly was nimble, and presently they came to the Bridge of One Hair, so called because it is the narrowest and lightest bridge in the world. Molly got across, but the giant could not; she stood on the other side, panting for breath, while he shook his fist at her and shouted:

> 'Get thee gone, Molly Whipple, get thee gone!—
> If once more thou cross my path,
> Thou shalt feel the giant's wrath!'

But Molly only brandished the great sword and called back:

> 'Twice again, old Fi-Foh-Fee,
> I shall come to trouble ye!'

Then she gave a merry laugh and ran off towards the King's palace. When she got there, the King was delighted to have the sword of his enemy, the cruel giant, and he gladly promised Molly's eldest sister the hand of his eldest son in marriage. And there was a solemn feast and great rejoicing.

'Now,' said the King to Molly, 'if you could get me the giant's purse, which lies under his pillow, I would promise my second son in marriage to your other sister.'

'Very well, Your Majesty,' said Molly with a curtsy, 'I will do what I can.'

So once more Molly went off alone to the giant's house,

and when it was dark, she crept in and hid under the bed. Before long the giant thumped his way in from supper, flung himself upon the bed, and began to snore like ten thunder-storms. Molly had no difficulty in slipping her hand under the pillow and pulling out the purse. But as she made her way with it towards the door, she tripped over and pulled down a great stone pot, and the noise of its fall woke the giant, who started up and sprang towards the door, just as Molly had darted through it. Well, the giant was a mighty runner, but Molly was nimble, and soon they came to the Bridge of One Hair, which the giant could not cross.

Molly stood on one side, and the giant stood on the other, and once more he shouted:

> 'Get thee gone, Molly Whipple, get thee gone!—
> If once more thou cross my path,
> Thou shalt feel the giant's wrath!'

And he shook his great hairy fist at her; but Molly only laughed and waved the purse at him, calling back:

> 'Once again, old Fi-Foh-Fee,
> I shall come to trouble ye!'

And with that she ran off and was gone in a flash.

When she got back to the King's palace, she gave the purse to the King, who was overjoyed. He at once made arrangements for the betrothal of his second son to Molly's elder sister, and a solemn feast was held amidst great rejoicing.

'Now,' said the King to Molly, when the ceremony was over, 'there is just one more thing I should like you to get for me. It will not be easy; and if you get it, you shall have the hand of my youngest son in marriage, as soon as you are old enough.'

'What must I get?' asked Molly.

'You must get,' said the King, 'the gold ring off the giant's finger.'

Well, Molly thought about the cruel giant, and then she thought about the handsome young Prince and how she would like to be a princess like her sisters, so she said she would try. Off she went that night, and when it was nearly dark, she slipped into the giant's house and hid under the bed. In a little while the giant thumped his way to bed, and his snoring was like the rumbling of twelve earthquakes. The moon shone through the window, and in the light of the moon Molly could see that the giant's hand was hanging over the side of the bed, and there was the gold ring, shining and sparkling. She put out her hand and took hold of it and gave it a pull. But the ring was stuck tight on the giant's finger, and the whole bed shook with the giant's snoring, and Molly herself was trembling with fear, so that she could hardly shift the ring an inch. But shift it she did, and just as she got it off, the giant gave a great shout, grabbed Molly by the hand in a terrible grip, and jumped out of bed. His fierce eyes shone in the moonlight, and his voice shook with anger.

'Aha, Molly Whipple!' said he. 'So I have caught thee at last, have I? Thou saidst thou wouldst come again, didst thou not?'

'Yes, sir,' said Molly in a tiny small voice.

'And I said thou shouldst feel the giant's wrath, did I not?'

'Yes, sir,' said Molly in an even tinier, smaller voice.

'Now then,' he said in a very quiet, determined tone, 'tell

me, Molly Whipple, since thou art so clever, if thou hadst caught me, what wouldst thou do to me, eh?'

'What would I do to thee?' asked Molly.

'Yes,' said the giant. 'Tell me that now, and be quick about it.'

'I'll tell thee what I would do,' said Molly. 'See that big bag that you have over there for bringing home your dinner in? Well, I would tie you up inside it, together with a cat, a dog, a needle and thread, and a pair of scissors.'

'Yes,' said the giant. 'What then?'

'Then,' said Molly, 'I would go out into the woods and cut me the biggest stick I could find, and I would beat you with it till you lost your senses.'

'So that's what you would do, is it,' said the giant, 'if you had me in your power, Molly Whipple? And that's just what I'm going to do with you. Into that bag with you, and as soon as it's daylight, I'm off to the woods to cut a stick to beat you with.'

So he picked Molly up and bundled her into the bag, together with a cat, a dog, a needle and thread, and a great pair of scissors. Then he tied the neck of the bag up tight, hung it on a nail in the wall, and went back to sleep. Inside the bag, Molly made friends with the cat and the dog, lay down as comfortably as she could, and waited till morning.

As soon as it was light, the giant stalked off into the woods, leaving Molly safely tied up in the bag.

Presently the giant's wife came in.

> *'Fee, fi, foh, fum,'*

said she, sniffing the air,

> *'I smell the blood of some earthly one.'*

'Giant's wife, giant's wife!' called Molly from inside the bag. 'Is that you?'

'What are you doing inside that bag?' asked the giant's wife.

'Oh, if only you could see what I see!' said Molly.

'And what can you see in there?' asked the giant's wife.

'Things you'd not believe,' answered Molly. 'If only you could see them too.'

'Let me in,' said the giant's wife, 'so that I can see what you see.'

So quickly Molly cut her way out with the scissors. She took the needle and thread with her and jumped down to the floor. Then she helped the giant's wife up into the bag and began sewing up the hole as fast as she could. She had just got the hole sewn up again when she heard the giant coming back. So she hid behind the door and waited. The giant strode into the room waving a whole tree which he had brought back from the wood.

'Now,' shouted he, 'where's that impudent girl? Let me get at her! Tie me up in a bag, would she, and beat me with a stick?'

He raised the great stick he had brought from the wood and began beating the bag with it as hard as he was able.

'It's me, not the girl!' shouted the giant's wife inside the bag. 'Let me out, can't you! Let me out!'

But the giant could not hear her, for the cat and the dog set up such a howling and a screeching that her voice was drowned. As for Molly, she crouched behind the door and watched; she did not feel at all sorry for the giant's wife, for she remembered how she had pretended to be kind to her and her sisters and then had opened the cupboard and given them away to her husband. But after a few moments she took her chance and slipped out of the house. Then she ran back to the King's palace and gave him the giant's ring.

The King was overjoyed to see her, for he was afraid that this time the giant might have been too clever for her; besides, she was such a bright, quick-witted girl that he knew she would make an excellent wife for his youngest son.

So Molly and the youngest of the princes were betrothed; and after some years, when they were of age to be married, a great and solemn wedding was held, amidst universal rejoicing. For the Prince was beloved by all the people, and Molly, by her quick wits and her brave defiance of the giant, had made herself equally beloved.

As for the cruel giant, after his magic sword, his purse, and his ring had been taken from him, he lost his power to do harm in the land; he pined and became melancholy, and soon was heard of no more. All the mothers and fathers for many miles around had cause to be grateful to Molly for ridding the country of the fierce giant who threatened the lives of all their children.

THE DONKEY, THE TABLE,
AND THE STICK

❖

There was once a boy called Robin, who lived in a cottage with his father. His father was a cross man and was not kind to his son. Poor Robin, though a good boy, was simple, and not very clever at the things that make boys admired by their fathers. He worked as hard as he could, doing odd jobs about the house and garden; but his father always scolded him when anything went wrong, and Robin was not happy.

But because he was good and simple, the neighbours liked the boy. He would say good day to them with a friendly smile as they passed him on the road, and was never too busy to give them a helping hand.

In a nearby cottage in the same village lived an old widow and her daughter Margaret. Margaret and Robin soon fell in love, and Robin asked his father if he might marry Margaret and bring her home as his wife.

'Marry,' said his father, 'marry? And how are you going to keep a wife, might I ask, when you can't even keep yourself? You don't expect *me* to provide for the both of you, I hope! Before you think of marrying, you'd best see if you can make

161

a decent living. Now, be off with you and hoe the cabbages, for they're nigh choked with weeds.'

Well, Robin thought over what his father had said, and one fine day in the spring he made up his mind to seek a fortune— or at any rate, if not a fortune, at least enough for him and Margaret to live on. He did not tell his father where he was going, for fear his father would try to stop him; besides, to tell the truth, he did not know where he was going. But it was a spring morning, he was young and strong, and what did anything else matter? He told Margaret, and the two of them said goodbye behind the widow's cottage, and Robin promised to come back in a year or less.

When he had got well clear of his own village, he began to ask for work. He told people he was seeking his fortune, and at that they just laughed and told him he would find no fortune thereabouts. He was beginning to think he would never find work to do, much less a fortune, when the road he was taking ran into a dark wood; and there he almost knocked down an old woman who was gathering sticks. The sticks dropped from her arms and fell all about the road.

'Oh, forgive me, ma'am,' said Robin. 'I'm truly sorry. Here, you rest yourself beside the road, and I'll pick up the sticks and carry them home for you.'

'You're a clumsy fellow,' said the old woman, 'but you mean no harm.'

Robin did not mind this, for he was used to being called clumsy. He soon had the sticks in a bundle again and was following the old woman back to her cottage.

'What do you do for a living, young man?' asked the old woman.

'Nothing, ma'am,' said Robin.

'Come, come,' said the woman, 'clumsy as you are, you must do *something*.'

Robin told her he was looking for work.

'What can you do?' she asked.

'Anything you ask,' said Robin.

'Well, if you will work for me as my servant,' said the old woman, 'I'll give you board and lodging, and at the end of a year I'll pay you well. You're a foolish boy, but strong, and I dare say you'll be willing enough.'

'Oh, that I will,' said Robin, 'and thank you, ma'am, to be sure.'

So he became the old woman's servant and worked as best he could for a year and a day. He cut wood, made the fire, dug the vegetable plot, fed the hens, washed the dishes, and in short, did everything except make his fortune.

'You have worked well,' said the old woman, 'and I promised to pay you. Here, take my donkey and get you gone.'

'Thank you, indeed, ma'am,' said Robin politely, wondering what in the world he would do with a donkey.

He couldn't eat it, he couldn't even feed it, but perhaps he could sell it. Anyway, there it stood, his wages for a year's work, a grey-brown, obstinate creature with two long ears and a face that looked as if it was trying to look wise.

'It's a very good donkey,' the old woman went on. 'Here; take hold of its ears and give them a good pull.'

Robin did as he was told. Grasping the donkey's two ears, he gave them a good pull. Instantly the donkey stopped trying to look wise and said, 'Ee-aw, ee-aw!' and a little shower of gold and silver pieces fell from its mouth.

'There,' said the old woman. 'That's not bad wages for a year's work. Now get along home, and don't lose the donkey on the way. Goodbye, and good luck to you.'

Without another word, and without waiting to be thanked, she made off into the cottage, leaving Robin standing in the road outside with his donkey. Robin pulled its ears once more, just to see if he was dreaming or not, and once more a shower of gold and silver dropped on the road at his feet.

'Gee up!' he cried, without even waiting to pick up the pieces, and off he went on the road for home.

Long before he was in sight of his own village, the night came on, so he decided to stay at an inn on the way. He stopped at the first comfortable-looking inn he came to and drove the donkey into the yard and tied him to a post.

'I'd like a bed for the night and a good meal,' he said, as soon as the landlord came out.

'Come inside,' said the landlord.

They went in. Then the landlord saw that Robin was a poor young fellow, not very well-dressed.

'I can let you have a meal and a bed,' said he, 'but you'll have to pay me for it first.'

'Gladly,' said Robin, 'wait just a minute, and I'll fetch you the money at once.'

He went out into the yard, gave the donkey's ears a pull, and was back in the inn half a minute later with a handful of silver.

The landlord took the money, gave Robin a hearty meal, and showed him to a fine room with a polished chest and a feather bed.

When Robin was settled for the night, the landlord stole

out to the yard. He had seen through a crack in the door how Robin had got the money, and he determined to steal the donkey. He led Robin's donkey away and locked him in a shed, and tied up in its place a donkey of his own.

Next morning, he asked Robin if he had had a good night, gave him breakfast, and showed him his road home.

'Don't linger on the way,' he said, 'and you'll be there by dinner-time.'

So Robin thanked him, took hold of the rope round the donkey's neck, clicked his tongue to make the creature start, and set off for home.

When he got home, his father was glad to see him; for although he had never been kind to the boy, he had missed him; besides, he was tired of doing all the odd jobs about the house himself.

'Welcome home,' he said. 'Where have you been?'

'Father,' said Robin, 'I have worked for a whole year and made my fortune. Now I've come home to ask your blessing on my wedding with Margaret.'

'Not so fast, not so fast. What's this about a fortune? Come, show me your wages.'

'This donkey is my wages,' said Robin.

'Is that all they gave you for a year's work? Well, you can't marry on that, boy, can you?'

'Not so fast,' said Robin. 'This is no ordinary donkey, Father. Here—just you pull his ears. That's right—give them a good strong pull.'

So the father did as he was told, and instead of giving him a shower of gold pieces the donkey turned round and bit his hand, and let him have a good kick on the shins into the bargain.

'Here, what kind of a trick is this?' said the father.

'I'm sorry, Father,' said Robin. 'Truly I am. This is not the donkey it was before.'

'Maybe it isn't. But you're the very same donkey you ever were, my son. You'd better go out and have another try at making your fortune. And when you come back next time, don't play spiteful jokes on your only father!'

Poor Robin, who, of course, knew nothing of how the thieving landlord had stolen his magic donkey, did not know what to say; so he went off to tell Margaret what had happened. She wished him better luck next time, and the following day he took his donkey by the halter and went off once more to seek his fortune.

Before the morning had passed, he came upon a carpenter trying to carry a heavy board into his workshop. Robin took hold of one end and gave him a hand.

'I'm looking for work,' he said. 'I'm not very clever, but I can saw and hammer, fetch and carry, sweep out the shed, and make myself handy in all sorts of ways.'

Now it happened that the carpenter was looking for just such a lad as Robin. He told him he would give him board and lodging for a year, and if at the end of that time he had worked well, he would give him his wages.

So once more Robin worked hard, morning, noon, and evening, for a year and a day, and at the end of that time the carpenter said he was well pleased and would give him his wages. So he fetched out a wooden table and set it before him.

'There,' said the carpenter, 'I think you'll be well pleased with that, for it's no ordinary table.'

Robin looked at it. It was a good enough table, but he couldn't think what in the world he would do with it.

'Just tell it to be covered,' said the carpenter.

'Table, be covered!' ordered Robin, and instantly there was a sort of flurry and a clatter in the air, and the table was covered with a wonderful dinner, the most splendid that Robin had ever seen. There was a roast turkey, potatoes, green peas, pudding and cream, and all manner of sauces and sweetmeats. Everything was on silver dishes, all clean and shining.

'It's just about dinner-time,' said the carpenter, 'so how about you and me sitting down and enjoying the good things the table has provided?'

So they sat down opposite one another, and never had Robin tasted such a meal in his life. Afterwards, the carpenter said, 'Now tell it to uncover itself.'

'Table,' said Robin, 'uncover yourself!'

Instantly there was a flurry and a clatter in the air, and all the dishes and the remains of the meal vanished, and the table was as bare and clean as before.

He thanked the carpenter, bade him good day, tied the table on the back of the donkey, and set out once more for home.

Night was coming on long before he was within reach of his own village, and coming upon the same inn where he had spent the night a year before, he decided to put up there again.

He asked the landlord if he could let him have a room for the night.

'Why, yes,' said the landlord, 'but I can give you little in the way of supper, for we have nothing in the house but some stale bread, a bit of cheese, and a mug of ale.'

'Never mind about that,' said Robin. 'Just you look here. Table,' he said, 'be covered!'

Once more there was a flurry and a clatter, and the table was full of good things to eat. The landlord and Robin sat down opposite one another, and when they had eaten their fill, Robin got rid of the dishes in the same way as before. The landlord thanked him for the meal, but made no remark on the table, for he had already determined to steal it, just as he had stolen the donkey.

When Robin was safely asleep, the landlord carried the wonderful table into a private room, and put an ordinary one, just like it to look at, in its place. Then he ordered a meal from the magic table, carried the dishes into the parlour and put them on the other table.

When Robin came downstairs to breakfast, the landlord told him he had already got the table to provide food and drink. So they sat down together. Robin said he must be away, for he was anxious to get home and show his father the table. He was just going to tell it to uncover itself when the landlord stopped him.

'If you don't mind,' he said to Robin, 'I'll just carry those dishes into the kitchen, for it's a pity to see such fine plates and mugs disappear; and the rest of the food will do for my old woman when she comes downstairs. Then you needn't pay for your night's lodging.'

Robin agreed to this, for he had no suspicion that the landlord had stolen his table. He helped him carry the remains of the meal into the kitchen. When the table was quite empty, he took it up and once more tied it on to the back of the donkey. He thanked the landlord for his hospitality and began to trudge along his homeward road. He sang as he went, for he had had a good night, the day promised to be fine, and he was looking forward to seeing Margaret once more, and even his father, whom he had not set eyes on for a whole year.

When he reached the cottage, his father was thinking about getting dinner ready.

'Welcome home,' said he. 'You're just in time to help me clean the vegetables and cook the bacon.'

'No, no,' said Robin. 'I've something better than that on the back of my old donkey here.'

He brought the table indoors and set it down in the middle of the room.

'My year's wages,' he said proudly. 'When you see what this table can do, Father, I don't think you'll stand in the way of my wedding with Margaret for, as you'll see, I shall now be able to provide for her for the rest of our days.'

'What are you talking about?' said the father. 'Is that common wooden table all they gave you for a year's work? I fear you'll never make a fortune, my boy, and as for marrying, you'd better make up your mind to be a bachelor till the day of your death.'

'Just you wait,' said Robin. 'Father, tell the table to be covered. Go on—just tell it.'

'Well, I suppose it can't bite me or give me a kick in the shins. Table, I say, table, be covered, do you hear!'

But of course nothing happened. Again and again poor Robin told the table to be covered, but all in vain, for, of course, this was no more than an ordinary table, just like any other.

Well, this time Robin's father was so angry that he drove the boy out of the cottage without even giving him any dinner, telling him to get himself work which was properly paid for. Off went the boy to see his sweetheart. She told him not to despair but to try once more, and this time he was certain to be lucky. They said goodbye, and for the third time Robin left his village in search of work.

He had not gone far when he saw a man trying to make a bridge over a stream. The man was chopping away at the trunk of a tree which grew by the water's edge. Robin offered to give him a hand.

'Can you use an axe?' asked the man.

'I can do better than that,' said Robin, and immediately began to climb the tree to the very top. When he was firmly seated among the highest boughs, he called down to the man to give the trunk a few more strokes of the axe. In a few moments the weight of Robin at the top of the tree brought it slowly down so that it lay right across the stream. Robin picked himself up, safe and sound, on the farther bank. The man thanked him for his help and said he would give him a reward. So saying, he cut off a short, stout stick from the tree and chopped off the twigs.

'There,' he said, 'I think that will be useful to you.'

Robin thanked the man and took the stick. It was an odd sort of reward, he thought, for if he wanted a stick, he could have cut one himself from the hedge as he went on his way.

'That's no ordinary stick, young man,' said the other. 'Just you tell it to start whacking.'

170

Robin held the stick out in front of him and said: 'Whack, stick, whack!'

Instantly the stick jumped out of his hand and began hitting the air violently—so violently that the man had to jump out of the way.

'There,' he said; 'now, if anyone tries to annoy you, you've got a very handy weapon. Take it, young man, and my blessing for your help.'

So Robin set off with the stick in his hand; and as he went on his way, a thought came into his head.

'What happened to that donkey?' he said to himself. 'And what happened to that table? They must have been stolen, and ordinary ones put in their place. Now the only person who could have seen me use them was the landlord at that inn. He was a sly-looking rascal, now I come to think of it, and I'll be bound he's got my donkey and my table stowed away somewhere.'

Well, the more he thought about it, the more certain he was that the landlord had stolen his property.

'I'll show him,' said Robin; and grasping his stick firmly in his hand, he strode along the high road until he came to the inn.

He banged on the door with the stick, opened it without waiting for an answer, and marched in.

The landlord came out of the kitchen to see who was making all the noise.

'You're the fellow I want,' said Robin. 'Do you remember me?'

'I can't say as I do,' said the landlord, looking craftily at Robin, 'but I expect you're somebody mighty important to walk in like that without so much as a by your leave.'

'You'll soon find out if I'm important or not,' said Robin. 'Now then, where's my donkey and my table that you stole from me when I spent the night in your rotten, thievish, rat-ridden inn? Fetch them out at once, or I'll give you a taste of my stick!'

'I know nothing about your donkey and your table!' roared the landlord. 'Instead of threatening honest folks like that, you'd better—'

But Robin didn't wait for him to finish.

'Oh, you don't know where they are, don't you? Then take that, you swindling old highway robber, you! Whack, stick, whack! Whack him sound and proper, do you hear!'

And just as if it *had* heard, the stick jumped up in the air and started to give the landlord the biggest thrashing he had ever had in his life. Over his back and shoulders it fell, round his ribs and legs, and on top of his head, till he ran out of the room howling. But the stick followed him—upstairs it flew and downstairs again, till the landlord lay on the floor, covering his face with his hands and shouting to Robin to call it off.

'I'll give you back your donkey,' he cried. 'I'll give you back your table, only fetch off this accursed stick, will you? I tell you, it's beating me to death! The donkey is in the shed at the end of the yard, and the table's upstairs in my wife's parlour. Call off this device of the devil, and I'll fetch them for you.'

So Robin told the stick to stop whacking and caught it firmly by one end. It stopped beating the landlord and lay still in his hand.

The landlord got up, rubbed his bruises and, still groaning and moaning, went upstairs and brought down Robin's table—the magic table; then he went round to the back of the inn and brought the magic donkey into the yard. Robin got the donkey to give him some gold pieces and the table to give him a meal, to make sure they really were his own possessions. Then he tied the table on the donkey's back, grasped his stick tightly in his right hand in case he met with thieves on the road, and set off without another word to the landlord.

And that was how Robin made his fortune. When he reached home, his father was truly glad to see him this time, for he brought money and good food with him. Robin forgave his father for his former hard-heartedness, and with money from the donkey, he bought him a bigger cottage in the middle of the village and hired him a servant to do the housework. As for Margaret, she was overjoyed to have Robin back again. It was not long before the two were married, and with the help of the table they were able to give the most splendid marriage-feast ever provided in the village. And then, for all I know, they lived happily ever afterwards.

THE WELL OF THE WORLD'S END

$$\text{◆}$$

Once upon a time, and a very long time ago it was, there was a girl called Rosemary. She was a good girl but not very clever, and a merry girl but not too pretty; and all would have been well with her but that she had a cruel stepmother. So instead of having pretty dresses to wear and sweet cakes to eat and idle friends to play with, as all girls should, she was made to do the housework: to go down on her knees and scrub the stone floors, and roll up her sleeves to the elbows and do the washing. And the better she did the work, the worse her stepmother hated her. If she got up early in the morning, it was not early enough; if she cooked the dinner, it was not cooked right. Poor Rosemary! She worked all the day, yet everything she did was wrong.

Well, one day her stepmother decided to be rid of her.

'Child,' said she, 'take this sieve and go to the Well of the World's End; and when you have found it, fill the sieve with water and bring it back to me. Mind now, and see that you don't spill a drop. Be off with you!'

So Rosemary, who never dared answer her stepmother

back, nor even ask her a question hardly, took the sieve and went out to look for the Well of the World's End.

Presently she met a carter, who had stopped to tighten his horse's reins.

'Where are you off to?' asked he. 'And what have you got in your hand?'

'I am trying to find the Well of the World's End,' she answered, 'and this is a sieve that I must fill with water.'

The carter laughed heartily and said she was a foolish girl and that he had no idea where the well was. So saying, he jumped back upon his cart, whipped up the horse, and left poor Rosemary standing in the road.

She walked on a while, and soon she saw three little boys bowling their hoops in the yard before an inn.

'Where are you off to?' one of them shouted. 'And what have you got in your hand?'

'I am trying to find the Well of the World's End,' she answered, 'and this is a sieve that I have to fill with water.'

All the three boys laughed aloud at this and told her she was stupid and that there was no such well in the world.

So Rosemary trudged on, asking everybody she met if they could tell her where the well was; but no one knew. Some were rude, some laughed at her, and others said they would have helped her if they could, but they knew not how.

At last she spied an old ragged woman, bent nearly double, looking for something in a cart-rut. She had a torn bonnet, very nearly no teeth at all, and a crooked stick. With this she was poking about in the mud.

'What are you looking for?' asked Rosemary.

'I had two groats that I was going to buy bread with, and if I don't find them, I shall have nothing to eat tonight.'

So Rosemary helped her look for the two groats, and presently her sharp eyes caught sight of them.

'Thank you,' said the old woman in her creaky voice. 'I should never have found them by myself, I do declare. Now tell me where you are going and what you are doing with that sieve.'

'I am going to the Well of the World's End,' said Rosemary, 'but I am afraid there is no such place in the world. When I get there, I must fill the sieve with water and take it home to my stepmother.'

'Why, indeed,' said the old woman, 'there is a Well of the World's End, and I will tell you how to find it. As for what you are going to do when you get there, that is another matter.'

So, pointing with her stick, she showed Rosemary the way.

'Through the gap in that hedge,' she said, 'over the far hill, up the stony path along the hazel wood, and along the valley—that will take you there. God speed you, and may the way seem short.'

Rosemary thanked her, and the old woman hobbled off, clutching her stick in one bony hand and her two groats in the other.

Through the gap in the hedge went Rosemary with her sieve, up the hill, along the stony path by the hazel wood, until she came to a deep valley, all wet underfoot, and very green and lonesome. And at the very end of the valley was a well. It was so overgrown with ivy and moss that she nearly missed it. But there it was, sure enough: and this was the Well of the World's End.

Rosemary knelt down on the bank beside the well, and dipped her sieve into the water. Many times she dipped it, but each time the water ran out through the holes in the sieve, so that not a drop was left to take home to her stepmother. She sat down and cried.

'I shall never do it,' she sobbed. 'I shall never have a sieveful of water to take home.'

Just as she was beginning to think that her misery would never end, something croaked, and a fat green frog hopped out from under a fern-leaf.

'What's the matter?' asked the frog.

Rosemary told him.

'If you promise,' said the frog, 'to do everything I ask for a whole night, I can help you.'

'Yes, of course I will,' said Rosemary eagerly. 'I'll promise whatever you like—only *do* help me, *please*.'

The frog considered for a moment or two, gulped once or twice, and spoke:

> *'Stop it with moss, and daub it with clay,*
> *And then it will carry the water away.'*

Quickly Rosemary gathered soft, green moss from the mouth of the well and covered the bottom of the sieve with it. Then she scooped up some damp clay from the bank and spread it on top of the moss, pressing it down until all the holes in the sieve were filled. Next, she dipped the sieve into the water, and this time not a drop ran out.

'I must get home as quickly as I can,' she said, turning to go. 'Thank you, thank you, dear frog, for helping me. I should never have thought of that for myself.'

'No, I don't suppose you would,' croaked the frog. 'Carry the water carefully—and don't forget your promise.'

Rosemary remembered that she had promised the frog to do anything he wanted for a whole night. She didn't suppose that any harm would come of a promise made to a frog, so she told him she would not forget, and went gratefully on her way.

You can imagine how surprised her stepmother was to see her when she got home. She had hoped to get rid of the girl for good and all. But here she was, none the worse for her journey, carrying a sieve full of water, just as she had been told. The stepmother didn't say much, because she was too angry. Instead, she made her get the supper for them both and wash the dishes afterwards, just as if nothing had happened.

As night was falling, they were surprised to hear the sound of knocking at the door.

'Who can it be?' asked the stepmother.

Rosemary went to the door and called out: 'Who's there, and what do you want at this time of day?'

There was a little croaking noise, and a voice said:

> 'Open the door and let me in,
> Let me in, my heart of gold;
> Remember the words we spoke so true
> Down by the water, green and cold.'

It was the frog. Rosemary had almost forgotten him. Her stepmother asked her who it was at the door, and Rosemary told her all about the frog and the promise she had made him.

'Well, let him in,' said the stepmother, 'and do as he tells you. Girls must keep their promises.'

She rather liked the idea of her stepdaughter's having to obey the commands of a frog. So Rosemary opened the door, and the frog hopped in. He looked at her, and then he spoke again. This is what he said:

> *'Lift me, lift me up to your knee,*
> *Up to your knee, my heart of gold;*
> *Remember the words we spoke so true*
> *Down by the water, green and cold.'*

Rosemary did not much like the idea of having a damp frog sitting on her knee, but her stepmother said:

'Do as he tells you. Girls must keep their promises.'

So the girl lifted the frog up, and he sat perched on her knee. Then, once more he spoke to her.

> *'Give me, O give me meat and drink,*
> *Meat and drink, my heart of gold;*
> *Remember the words we spoke so true*
> *Down by the water, green and cold.'*

'Do as he tells you,' ordered the stepmother. 'Girls must keep their promises.'

Rosemary fetched from the larder the food that had been left from supper and put it on a plate in front of the frog, and he bent his head down and ate every scrap of it. Then once more he spoke:

> *'Take me, take me into your bed,*
> *Into your bed, my heart of gold;*
> *Remember the words we spoke so true*
> *Down by the water, green and cold.'*

'No,' said Rosemary, 'I will never have such a cold, clammy creature in bed with me. Get away, you nasty animal!'

At this the stepmother almost screamed with laughter.

'Go on!' she cried. 'Do as the frog bids. Remember your promise. Young girls must keep their promises.'

With that she went off to her room, and Rosemary was left with the frog. Well, she got into bed, took the frog in beside her, but kept him as far away as she could. After a while she slept soundly.

In the morning, before the break of day, she was awakened by a croaking sound close to her ear.

'Everything I have asked, you have done,' said the frog. 'One more thing I ask, then you will have kept your promise. Take an axe and chop off my head!'

Rosemary looked at the frog, and her heart went cold.

'Dear frog,' she said, 'don't ask me to do that. You have been so kind to me. Don't ask me to kill you.'

'Do as I ask,' said the frog. 'Remember your promise. The night is not yet over. Fetch an axe, and cut off my head.'

So very sadly Rosemary went into the kitchen and fetched the chopper that was used to cut up logs for the fire. She could scarcely bear to look at the poor frog, but somehow she managed to raise the chopper and cut off his head.

Then she had the greatest surprise of her life. For the frog was no more: in his place stood a young and handsome man. She stepped back in amazement, dropping the chopper to the floor. The young man was smiling at her.

'Don't be afraid,' he said in a soft and musical voice. 'I am not here to hurt or alarm you. Once I was a prince, but a foul enchantress turned me into a frog; and her wicked spell could not be unspelled until a young girl should do my bidding for a whole night.'

At these words the stepmother, who had been woken up by the sound of voices, came into the room. Great was her astonishment to see the young Prince there, instead of the slimy frog.

'Madam,' said the Prince, 'your daughter has had the kindness to unspell the spell that made me a frog; for that I am going to marry her. I am a powerful prince, and you shall not deny me. You wanted to get rid of your stepdaughter. Well, you have done so, for now I am going to take her away to be my wife.'

For once, the stepmother had nothing to say. She looked at the Prince and opened her mouth, but no words came; then she looked at Rosemary and opened her mouth, but still no words came. So she turned away and began to get some breakfast for them all. It was the only thing she could do.

Not long afterwards the Prince and Rosemary were married, and very happy they were. As for the stepmother, she had tried to get rid of her daughter, so that she had the pleasure of knowing that by this means she had caused her to rescue the Prince from enchantment and find herself a kind and loving husband.

DICK WHITTINGTON
AND HIS CAT

——— ❖ ———

O nce upon a time, more than five hundred years ago, there lived, in a country village, a poor orphan boy named Dick Whittington. Seeing that both his parents were dead and that he was so poor, the people of the parish gave him food and clothing and much kindness. But they were not rich themselves, so Dick had only the simplest of food and the most homely of clothing. When he heard of the great city of London with its towers and churches and its streets paved with gold—for that is what the people of the village said—he had a great longing to go and see it. But, of course, he had no idea how a poor village boy such as he would ever travel all that way to the city of London.

Now one day there was a jingling of bells in the village street, and a huge hay-wagon drawn by two horses pulled up at the inn. The wagoner got down to refresh himself and his horses, and Dick, seeing that he was friendly, fell to talking with him.

'Where are you going to?' asked Dick.

'Why, London town, to be sure,' said the wagoner.

'That must be a wonderful place,' said the boy. 'How I should like to go there!'

The wagoner saw how eager Dick was, and after he had talked to the good people with whom Dick was staying, he offered to take him to London on his wagon, to look after him while he was in London, and bring him back the next time he passed through that village. So Dick put his few belongings in a bundle and joined the wagoner on the seat behind the two horses. Then the wagoner cracked his whip, there was a jingling of bells, and they set off on the road to London.

When they reached the city, Dick looked about him, and saw the great houses and the tall churches but, above all, he looked for the streets paved with gold. For he had seen two or three golden crowns in the village at home, and he knew they were worth a great deal; so he thought that he would only have to stoop down and scrape and chip some pieces of gold from the pavements to make himself rich enough to live comfortably and have decent clothes, good food, and perhaps a snug cottage or a shop. Besides, he would be able to repay all the people of his parish who had been so good to him.

The wagon pulled up at an inn in the city, and while the driver went inside, Dick jumped down from the seat and began to look round. He was sure that those golden streets were just round the corner. But they were not, so he explored a little farther, and a little farther; and, to make a long story short, he lost himself and could not find his way back to the wagon. Evening came on, and poor Dick was so tired that he crept into a corner and curled up on a doorstep and went to sleep.

Next morning, he began to walk the streets looking for all the wonderful sights he had been told about. But he saw little more than streets of brick houses and poor people on their way to work. Presently he began to feel very hungry and was forced to beg halfpence from the passers-by. Most of them had little to give him except unkind words. Many asked why he did not seek for work. So when he had spent his few halfpence on bread and milk he started asking where he could get employment, so as to earn board and lodging.

He trudged wearily about until he came to some fields at the edge of the city, and there he found a farmer who was willing to give him, in exchange for his services as haymaker, his food and drink and a pile of straw in a shed where he could spend the night. The work was hard, but he was well-fed and comfortable. At last, however, haymaking was over, and the farmer had no more work for him. So back he tramped, along the streets of the city looking for more work. For three days he did this, but he had no luck. No one would employ him or give him so much as a crust of bread to keep him from starvation. At length, worn out and fainting from sheer exhaustion, he sank down upon a doorstep and fell asleep.

The door belonged to the house of a rich merchant, Mr Fitzwarren, who had made a great fortune by trading with distant lands. When Mr Fitzwarren's cook opened the door, she saw Dick huddled there in his rags, and roused him up with her broom; for she was a sour, cruel woman, and could not abide the sight of a ragged, dirty vagabond.

'Get you gone, you idle, loafing brat!' she cried. 'What are you doing on a respectable gentleman's threshold, I should like to know? Looking out for a chance to sneak something, I dare say!'

Poor Dick had no strength to answer, but struggled to his

185

feet, only to drop down once more on the pavement, for he was nearly dead from starvation. Just at that moment the merchant himself, Mr Fitzwarren, returned home. He was a kind-hearted gentleman, and was distressed to see Dick in such a wretched condition at his doorway. He asked Dick why he did not go home or return to his master, and when he learnt from the broken words which escaped the boy's lips that he had neither home nor master, he ordered the cook to take him in, give him food and clean clothing, and allow him to stay in the house as long as he needed.

When Dick had eaten and rested, Mr Fitzwarren saw that he was a decent, well-grown lad, though thin and weak from lack of food, and he ordered that he should be given work as a scullery-boy. The cook did not hold with this, for she had taken a dislike to Dick, but she was obliged to obey her master's orders.

Dick got on well enough in spite of the cruel cook, who never lost the opportunity of tormenting him in little ways, like spilling hot, greasy water over his feet and giving him all the unpleasant jobs to do. But the merchant's daughter, Alice, took pity on Dick, for she was a sweet-natured girl and liked the look of the orphan. So she told the cook that if she went on being unkind to Dick, she would see that her father dismissed her from his service. After this, the cook contented herself for the most part with saying unkind and spiteful things to Dick whenever no one was listening.

Now it happened that Dick had been given a bare and chilly garret to sleep in, and there were holes in the walls through which rats and mice came at night and woke him up from sleep. They scampered over his bed, and nibbled at his fingers if they happened to be showing outside the bed-clothes. From time to time, Alice gave him little presents, and one day she gave him a penny. He went out into the street, and there he saw a girl carrying a black cat in her arms.

'How much will you take to sell your cat?' he asked.

'I don't know that I want to sell him,' answered the girl. 'He is a very good mouser.'

'Oh, please let me have him,' asked Dick. 'A good mouser is exactly what I want.'

'Well, how much will you give me for him?' asked the girl.

'I have only a penny in the world,' said Dick, 'but that I will gladly give you if you will sell me the cat.'

Well, the girl took pity on Dick, even though she did not really want to sell Puss; so she took Dick's penny and gave him the cat. Dick kept him in his garret and fed him on scraps of food and saucers of milk, which he saved from his own meals and took secretly upstairs from the kitchen. And very soon Puss had chased away all the rats and mice, and Dick was able to sleep in peace. Dick and his cat grew very fond of each other, and when he was not watching the mouse-holes in the floor, Puss would curl up on the end of Dick's bed and keep himself warm. One day, Mr Fitzwarren called all his servants together and told them he was sending a new venture to sea and they might all join in, if they liked. His ship was going to the Barbary Coast laden with a cargo of goods to exchange for precious merchandise. All the servants might send something of their own with the ship and take their due share of the profits when it returned. Some sent jewels and trinkets, others sent dresses, and others sent money which they had saved out of their wages. Only Dick did not appear before his master, for he alone had nothing to send on the voyage. But Alice noticed that he was not there, so she sent for him and asked him if he, too, would like to risk something with the venture. Dick told her he had nothing at all to send, so Alice said she would give him some money. But her father said that every servant must send something of his own; it could not be given him by another. Then Alice thought of Dick's cat and told him to send that.

'Very well,' said Dick, though the idea of parting from Puss made him very sad. 'I will send Puss if you think he will be of any use.'

'Of course he will,' cried Alice eagerly. 'He will keep the rats and mice out of the ship.'

So Dick said goodbye to his cat, and next day the cat was taken aboard the ship, which soon set sail for the Barbary Coast.

The loss of his cat made Dick very unhappy, and once more the rats and mice began to keep him awake at night, so that he was sometimes late for work in the morning. His friend Alice went away to stay in the country for a while, and the unkind cook once more began to treat Dick with cruelty. Not only did she show him every possible unkindness, she even sneered at him about his cat.

'Fancy sending a creature like that on a voyage!' she said. 'Why, how much do you think *he*'ll sell for? Just about enough to buy a stick to beat with, I should say.'

At last Dick could stand it no longer. He had lost his cat, he had lost his friend and protector Alice, and the cook was once more as unkind to him as ever. So he packed his few small belongings in a handkerchief and set out upon the road one morning as soon as it was light. It was the morning of All Hallows' Day, and soon he reached Highgate, where he sat down by the roadside and wondered which way to go. All roads were the same to him, and he could not make up his mind. Then, all at once in the silent morning air, he heard the sound of far-off bells. They were the bells of Bow Church in Cheapside, and as Dick listened to them, they seemed to be speaking to him; and this is what they said.

> *'Turn again, Whittington,*
> *Thou worthy citizen.*
> *Turn again, Whittington,*
> *Lord Mayor of London!'*

Over and over again the bells seemed to be saying the same thing.

'Lord Mayor of London!' repeated Dick to himself. 'Well, if that's what is in store for me, there's hope yet.' So he stood up, shouldered his bundle, turned round to face the way he had come, and began to tramp back towards the city. On and on he went, the sound of Bow Bells still ringing in his head, until he reached his master's house. The household was beginning to stir, and Dick managed to creep indoors unnoticed and begin his day's work, just as the cook was coming down the stairs to get breakfast ready.

Meanwhile, poor Dick's cat was making himself useful on board Mr Fitzwarren's ship, the *Unicorn*. The voyage was a long one, and there were rats and mice among the cargo, but Puss chased them to their holes and killed as many as he could. Soon the captain and all the crew knew what a fine and clever cat he was.

189

At last they reached the Barbary Coast, where the brown-skinned Moors live. The ship put in to a harbour, and the captain was told that he must go and pay his respects to the King, who reigned in that part of the country. There was great excitement among the Moorish people at the waterside, for most of them had never set eyes on white people before.

The captain of the *Unicorn* was led to the royal palace, past the tall black guards, and into the presence of the King. The King told him he might bring his goods to the royal palace, where he would examine them and see whether he wished to buy them. Then he was led into a great dining-hall, where a banquet had been prepared in his honour. The King and Queen, the captain of the ship, and the people of the royal household sat down upon the cushions and rugs which lay upon the floor, for such was the custom of the country. No sooner had the servants brought the rich dishes of spiced meat, rice, and fruit, and placed them before the guests, than there was a scurrying sound from behind the curtains, and out ran a great horde of rats which began to devour the food upon the dishes. They took little notice of the servants who tried to chase them away, and it was with the greatest difficulty that any of the ladies and gentlemen were able to take food.

'What a great nuisance these rats must be to your majesty,' said the captain. 'Are you often plagued in this way?'

'Sir,' said the King of Barbary with a sigh, 'every meal-time is the same. My wise men and doctors have been consulted, but there is no remedy against these monsters. I would give the half of my wealth to anyone who could rid me of this pest.'

'In England,' said the captain, 'there is a little creature who is kept in our homes especially for killing and eating rats. It is called a cat. Have you no cats in this country?'

The King asked him to describe the creature, but no one had heard of anything like it in Barbary. He asked where a cat might be found.

'We have *one*, Your Majesty,' answered the captain, 'on board my ship; but, of course, he is a most valuable animal, for we have rats and mice among the ship's stores, and he is the only means of keeping them down.'

'Ah, what would I not give to possess that creature!' sighed the King. 'He would be a great blessing to me and all my household.'

'Well,' said the captain, who had an eye to business, and knew that the King of Barbary was a fabulously wealthy man—'well, Your Majesty, what *would* Your Majesty give?'

The King considered.

'Bring him to my palace this evening,' he said, 'and let us see what he can do. If he can perform what you say he can, I will make you an offer.'

Well, that same evening the captain carried Puss carefully under his arm to the royal palace and was once more admitted to the banqueting-hall. Another feast was about to begin. As soon as the food was set down by the servants, the rats rushed upon it from all sides. But Puss did not have to be told what to do. He sprang from the captain's grasp, leapt straight at the nearest rat, a large brown fellow who was in the act of carrying off a piece of meat and killed him instantly. The same fate befell a dozen more of the thieves, and the rest scuttled off behind the curtains and appeared no more. The King, the Queen, and all the royal household looked on in amazement.

'Well,' said the King of Barbary, 'if I had that creature, there would not be a rat in the palace in a week's time.'

'Indeed, my dear,' said the Queen, 'you must have him. Indeed you must. Offer this brave captain whatever he wants.'

So the King offered to buy the whole cargo of the *Unicorn* for a fair price, and in addition to give ten times this sum for the cat. The captain considered this a handsome offer, and one well worthy of such a great ruler, so he accepted it without argument.

Next day, the whole crew were feasted at the palace, the cargo was brought on shore and sold in exchange for gold and jewels, and a special casket of exceedingly rare and precious stones was given to the captain in exchange for Puss. Then the ship once more set sail and made for England.

One fine morning, Mr Fitzwarren, the London merchant, was seated in his counting-house when there came a knock at the door.

'Good news! Good news for Mr Fitzwarren!' said a voice, and in came the captain of the *Unicorn*, followed by the mate, bearing a heavy casket and a paper showing the contents of the ship.

'Your ship is come home, sir,' said the captain. 'This is what we have brought back from the coast of Barbary.'

The merchant welcomed the captain, ordered wine to be fetched for him and the mate, and examined the list of goods they had brought back. Then the captain told Mr Fitzwarren about Dick Whittington's cat, and opened the casket of jewels which the King of Barbary had given in exchange for him.

Pleased as the merchant had been with the success of his own venture, he was even more pleased at Dick's good fortune.

He turned to one of his servants.

'Send for Mr Whittington at once,' he said.

Dick was, at that moment, cleaning pots for the cook, and he was covered with grease and smuts; but just as he was, he obeyed his master's summons. When the merchant ordered a chair to be placed for him and told him to sit down, he was afraid that he was being made fun of. But Mr Fitzwarren told him what had happened, gave him his great riches, and begged him to keep them in a place of safety.

Dick begged his master to take a share in the jewels on account of his kindness to him, but Mr Fitzwarren refused.

'No,' he said, 'it is all yours, and I wish you joy of it. As for me, I have all I want; and it gives me great happiness to see you so fortunate.'

Then Dick tried to give part of his wealth to Miss Alice, who had always been kind to him and taken his part, but she would have none of it. So Dick gave the ship's captain and the mate and all his fellow servants—even the cruel cook— handsome presents all round, for he was not one to keep all his fortune to himself. And they all thanked him, and drank his health and wished him success.

Dick bought himself good clothes from a tailor, and when he was clean and neat and well dressed, he was as handsome a young fellow as any in the city of London. Mr Fitzwarren begged him to stay on in his house until he could find one for himself; and presently he began to see that his daughter Alice and young Dick Whittington had grown fond of each other. Dick had always given Alice such presents as he could afford, and she had always been kind and loving towards him. So, to make a long story short, Dick Whittington and Alice Fitzwarren were married soon afterwards, and a great wedding-feast was held, to which the Lord Mayor of London, the sheriff, and the aldermen were invited. They lived in a house of their own in great style and comfort, and Mr Whittington became one of the most popular and prosperous citizens in the town.

Not long afterwards, so history tells us, he became sheriff and was knighted by the King of England; and three times Sir Richard Whittington became Lord Mayor of London. And each time he was chosen Lord Mayor, he thought of that All Hallows' Day, many years before, when he sat by the roadside wondering where in the world to go; and the sound of Bow Bells had come to him through the clear winter air, and they had sounded like voices saying to him:

> *'Turn again Whittington,*
> *Thou worthy citizen.*
> *Turn again, Whittington,*
> *Lord Mayor of London!'*